NIKE

A NOVEL BY

CARA HOFFMAN

FACTORY SCHOOL

ITHACA & SAN DIEGO

2004

ISBN 0-9711863-5-9

The author gratefully acknowledges the support of the New York State Foundation for the Arts for a fellowship in fiction in 2000, The Saltonstall Foundation for studio space in the fall of 2002, and The New York State Council on the Arts and Community Arts Partnership of Tompkins County for a grant in 2003.

Factory School
Box 6709, Ithaca, New York 14850

For more information about this book, please visit
nike.factoryschool.org

NIKE

A NOVEL BY

CARA HOFFMAN

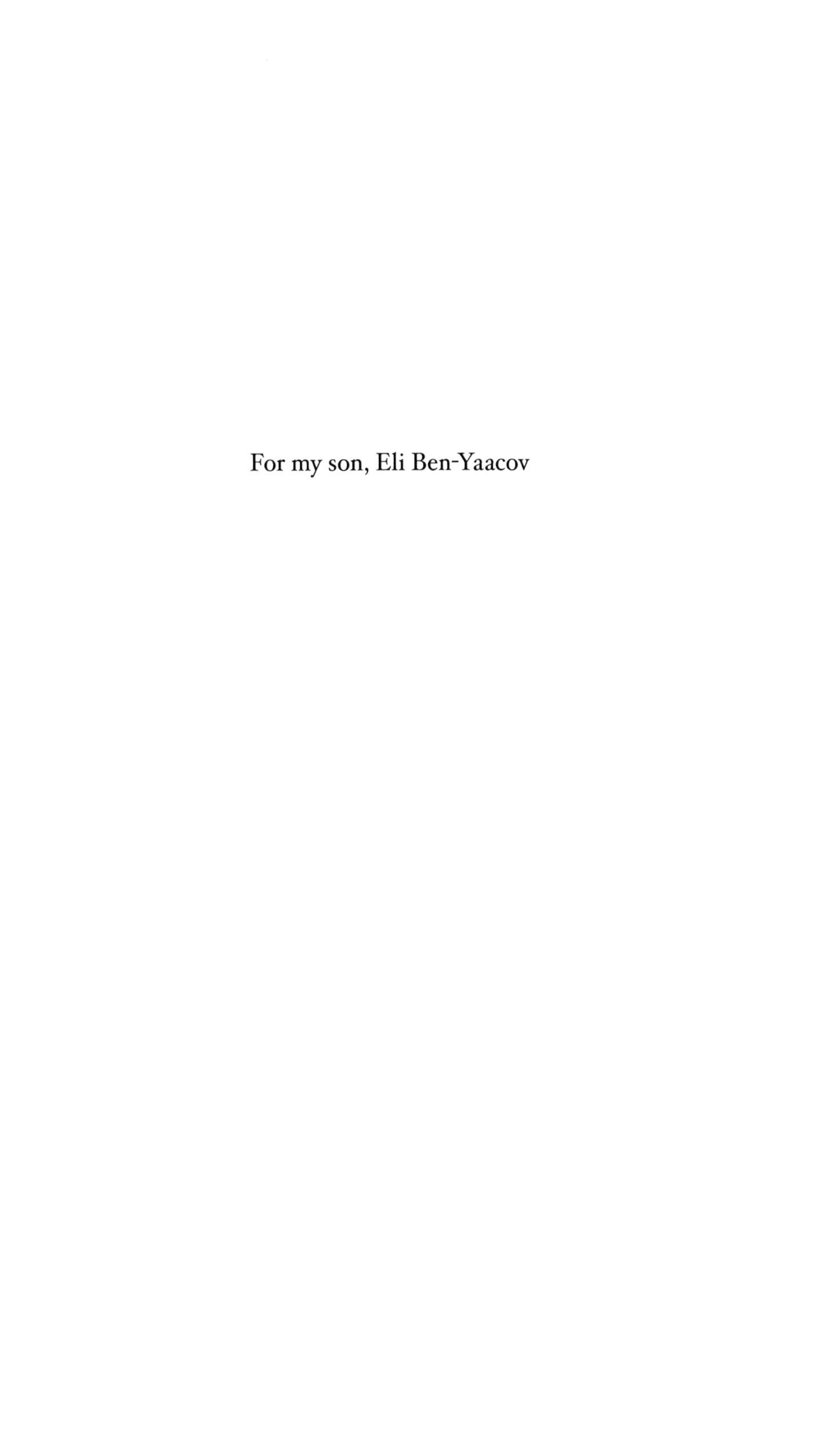

For my son, Eli Ben-Yaacov

Nothing is real there.
The ghost's existence, if it can be called that
is like a miserable dream.

Edith Hamilton
Timeless Tales of Gods and Heroes

1989

1

JEZZ DIED a week before I returned to Athens, so I never saw him again. I was told his parents arrived on what might have been the third day he was unconscious, dragged him down the spiral staircase, and drove away, probably to a hospital or maybe straight to the airport. Two days later he died in London of kidney failure or blood poisoning or some other unnecessary diagnosis. I don't know who was there when it happened, or who found out he was dead, but there was an obituary floating around so it was believable enough. It was believable even without the obituary, but I guess it was proof that he didn't just leave Athens like the rest of us.

Despite appearances, the rest of us must have had limits. The rest of us must have known or somehow sensed when we had wandered off the set.

But not Jezz.

When I left Israel, I believed that I was going back for him, for some notion of him that still assaulted my senses. For some look he had had. For some words he had said. For some promise I'd never have been stupid enough to make. Not even at eighteen.

*

"I've seen worse," said David at the end of the story. He shrugged and ran the tips of his fingers over his scalp. And then he started telling me about his trip to Yugoslavia, which, he thought, was far more interesting than Jezz in a coma, or Jezz dead.

"Look at it this way," he said brightly. "There's a job opening at Olympos now. You can get your old job back, even your old room back."

"Yeah, I'll have to do that. I'll do that today."

"And don't look so upset."

"Do I look upset?"

"You surely do," he said. "It looks awful."

Diligianni Street smelled like burning tar and oil with an occasional breeze of pastry coming from a shop doorway. Olympos was a four-dollar-a-night hotel at the end of Diligianni, across from Larissis train station and transvestite park. It was an older building, covered with years of exhaust but it stood apart from the other buildings that lined Athens' streets, the low white concrete structures, which were indistinguishable without numbers.

I walked up the cracked stairs to the lobby and saw Sterious sitting behind the front desk. He was a seventy-year-old man with faded tattoos showing above the collar of his shirt and on his fore arms. He had been a sailor in the Greek navy. For thirty years he traveled from Pireaus to Haifa to New York. But now he sat behind this desk, mostly drunk. Dimitri, the night receptionist, used to say; "Sterious is a-a-a m-monster! He is a Frank a Fr-frankenstein He-he-he..." He stuttered, Dimitri.

Nevertheless, Sterious the monstrous sailor sat behind the desk, and looked genuinely happy to see me. He grabbed both my hands and held them, speaking slowly and peering through his horn-rimmed glasses at my face.

"Maya, My-Yah. Where were you?"

"I was in Israel. Did you miss me?"

"Did you get pregnant?"

"No."

"Those Jews. Thirty years I sailed there."

"Uhuh." Sterious liked to talk about Jews.

"For more years than you've been alive I sailed there. Everyone now is a Jew in Palestine. Don't tell me it isn't so!"

"I wouldn't worry about it."

"How long do you stay?" he asked.

"I need work."

"Yes, Yes, you got work. But how long do you stay?"

We stared at each other. His eyebrows were arched and he was completely still.

"Three months you stay at least," he decided, placing my hands on the desk, and turning slowly to look at the board of hooks behind him.

He handed me the key to room thirty-one, all the way up the spiral staircase.

"Jezz went back to England," he said, and looked away. He was eager to tell me all about it, and it looked like it was making him feel bad.

"I know. I heard."

"Maybe he got of a fight with Jack, I don't know. Jack leaved first, very angry."

"Mmm."

"Jack's not like a man. He mope around and cry. You first think what a big strong nigger. But he's like a girl how he look at things. You know how a girl is—she think about things and then mope, maybe cry? But he's handsome, Jack."

"Mmm." Sterious liked to talk about "the niggers" too.

"You ignore me," he said slowly. "You. Don't. Ignore me. I'm old man with job for you. Hey! You don't ignore a old man."

"I'm not."

"Now, did you get pregnant from a Jew or no?"

"Jesus Christ!"

"Okay," he held up his hands in front of his face and looked over his shoulder.

I started for the stairs and he began talking very quickly.

"His parents come, you know, they think he's sick maybe but I don't know, I think..." he looked at my face and something made him change his demeanor and then lie. "You find him back home," he said. "Look him up...he's just liking boys for now, it happens a lot. All the time it happens. He likes you again soon. Hey, they buyed me these Turkish cups from the Plaka, eh?" He held up a red and gold demitasse cup. "Jack and Jezz buyed them," he smiled at me and I smiled back and nodded, looked at the cup.

This is what people do to you. They think their fantasies will save you. Like you can just step into it and say, 'ah, thank you, yes, somewhere Jezz is alive, but has a cold maybe. Maybe he's gone back to London. Maybe he's playing with the symphony. I see from your pitying smile that everything is just fine. Thank God I didn't really waste the only money I saved on a deck class ticket, to attend a drunk's wake, in the filthiest city in Europe. Because now, that would mean something, wouldn't it?'

"Start tonight. Catch the 309. I tell everyone you are back."

"Okay," I said starting up the stairs.

"Maya," he called after me. "What did you do in Palestine?"

"I picked fruit."

"Yes, you look a little bigger," he said, and went to fix his coffee.

*

The room was our old room, the room I shared with and Jack and Jezz. The walls were yellow and peeling and there was a little wrought iron balcony full of dirt and crushed glass with a gray washline hanging from end to end. The ceiling was high, molded tin painted blue. There were two beds and a cracked white sink with a mirror above it too high for me to see myself in.

I stood in front of the sink with the water running. I put my head under the faucet and let the water rinse the sweat off my neck and out of my hair. It was July, and by August it would already be up to one hundred and ten degrees of grimy city heat. You could feel it in your lungs. It was hotter outside than inside your body. And dry.

I pulled the bag off my shoulder and put it on the bed. It was small and black, and it had everything in it; a carton of Camels and a lighter from the duty free in Cypress, my passport, two thousand drachmas, a pair of jeans, two pairs of cut-offs, t-shirts, towel, soap, toothbrush, and a wool sweater. That was what I had left after two years of traveling.

I looked under the beds for anything that Jezz might have left: books, comic books, a t-shirt, maybe money...there was nothing. It was astounding how much nothing there was. I lay down on one of the thin mattresses and looked up at the bare bulb hanging from the ceiling.

This was the room where we had slept together in the heat. The room that spun beneath us while we played gin and hearts. Where we'd sit at night in our underwear getting up to drink from the short tap in the cracked sink.

This was the room where everything looked silver, at a certain time of night, with the dark gray sky shining in; moonless, starless, pale iridescence spilling through the balcony doors and washing everything. So that nothing was ugly. So that maybe nothing would ever be ugly again. The faded paint, the bare bulb, the scuffed walls and floors, were infused with clarity and gentleness, not worn or neglected. That light lay itself down upon our skin. It shone in the wetness of our eyes. And brought out the beauty of proximity. The beauty of faces, mouths, collarbones, a lip tucked beneath a lip. That light illuminated our sweat darkened hair. It revealed limbs and lines of a body traced back to the shadowed places of another body; the back of a knee, the curve of a hand, a fist closing around a wrist, or around an ankle, a fist closing around things that fit in the cradle between palm and fingers.

And at those times the hush of traffic going by sounded like an ocean lapping. I remembered now how beautiful their hands looked, in that room clasped in the silver light while they slept. Their cheeks upon the pillow when it was over and morning came up outside, turning the sky the color of an old bruise.

I lit a cigarette and watched the ceiling fade and tried not to remember why I was back in that room again.

2

The foundry passed slowly with the rhythm of the train, enormous and beautiful in the dark. The stacks of the building rose solid and black, beneath the white and yellow fire, visible only in contrast to the light. The stacks were like water. Like water at night. I folded my leaflets and wrote the prices across the top near the slogan "Get Ready to be Amazed!" The most expensive room was twelve hundred drachmas, which is about seven dollars. The least expensive was eight hundred. And tourists could sleep on the roof in their sleeping bags for about a buck.

I finished folding and stared out the window again. Outside, the ruins of the past thirty years lay, refusing to decay. Dark motionless figures lit by the moon. I remembered this countryside. It hadn't changed since I last saw it. Piles of tires, plastic bags and bottles, dead goats, and large dismembered pieces of machinery lay strewn about the landscape. Things fell into ruin quickly and remained that way forever, instead of enduring or suddenly being taken by catastrophe.

I was practically alone in the car with the exception of a few men commuting back to Elephsina for the evening. The conductor came around and grabbed my ticket. He had shiny black hair and a foul expression. They hated runners, and I was obviously a runner, even though I wasn't in the bar car.

I don't know why they call it running, it's more like waiting. Waiting for the train, then waiting for it to get you there, waiting for the alcohol to take affect so you don't mind lying to people, then waiting some more. Idling, not running. Idling in the bar car or at the station.

But I wasn't in the bar. I wasn't looking for anyone. I would see them all soon enough if they were still in the country. And I wasn't done thinking yet, didn't need company.

Some twisted silhouettes of an olive tree brushed by the window, and the carriage door opened in front of me. David walked in.

"You can kiss your commission goodbye lass, everyone's crying tonight. I'm on the train."

"I thought you weren't running."

"Of course I'm running."

He sat down across from me. "And you can put out that cigarette. It's a dirty antisocial habit." He took out a package of cookies, opened it and handed me one. "Woman, you look like a pile of rags." He continued staring intensely at my cigarette. "You've lost even more weight. Were they not feeding you in the Holy Land?"

"You asked me that last time you saw me."

"So I did."

"Sterious said I gained weight."

He shook his head, frowned. "Not at all. The man's a gobshite."

David was fifty-six years old, though he looked like he was in his thirties. He had shaved his head completely bald which made his eyes seem more intense and aggressive. They were very dark blue. His face had lines of definition but no wrinkles. He was not handsome, but he was insanely fit, having been in the military his entire life. He had lived in Athens for the last nine years because crimes he had committed as a mercenary prevented him from returning to Ireland. The names David, Seamus, Joseph, and Tommy were tattooed on his right forearm in blurry blue ink. And across his entire back was tattooed an eagle which had long since faded to green.

"Are you not listening to me?"

"What?" I asked. "I was thinking."

"I said you'd better snap out of it."

"Just a little culture shock, my dear."

"None such thing exists, my dear." He handed me another cookie. "You've got no reason to act this way. Not when I'm here. In a week you'll...."

He stopped talking abruptly as the train pulled in and he stood straight and silent, surveying the station from the window. Then we walked quickly through the car and down on to the platform, and the train pulled away while our backs were to it.

There were at least thirty runners waiting for the 309 outside a little shack that served as the station house. They were passing bottles of retsina and Metaxa around and talking. The train would be an hour late at the very least. I sat down next to some British kids. Blond hair, big boned, horrible teeth, drinking, waiting. All the fucking same.

"Hey when'd you get back?" asked some washed out boy whose

name I couldn't remember. He handed me a bottle and rolled the screw cap back and forth in his hands nervously.

"Today," I said, drinking from his Metaxa.

"Did you hear about Jezz and Black Jack?"

"You mean Jack Rollock. No."

"They were your mates weren't they?"

"No," I lied.

"They were poofs you know?" he laughed.

I said nothing.

"Can you believe it? Black Jack, eh? eh? Th'man's huge. Jezz y'could see, but Flak Jacket? Jesus-fuck. Nah."

I shrugged. I could picture Jack's face and I didn't want to. I made it go away by singing the Doublemint gum commercial in my head, until I realized it had the lines 'double your pleasure, double your fun...' in it. This of course, was hilarious. After a time I forgot what that oaf beside me had been talking about altogether. I had a vague sense that it wasn't good, but he still had more brandy left.

David was surrounded by a crowd of drunken admirers. Younger boys mostly, who would never claim they knew him, and would try to be clever just like him. The kind of boy who is slow, easy to shake off and quick to scare. They laugh before they've heard the joke, which is what they were doing tonight. Drunk and eager to sit through another hour of psycho commentary. Tales from the front. David wasn't drinking though. He never drank.

"We had to mutilate them," I overheard. "I mean, after we saw what they did to those nuns we couldn't very well let...." He gestured, one fist closed sliding gently through the air.

"When are you going back to London?" the kid asked. His face was now in front of mine, his body leaning out to the side. Nothing in this world is uglier than a boy in his early twenties.

"I'm not," I said. "I'm not from London."

"I thought you were his girl from way back."

"No. I hardly knew him. I didn't know him, didn't know either of them."

He seemed amused. "Are you English?"

"Do I sound English?"

He shrugged.

Now his Metaxa was burning my stomach, so I went to buy a pint of Amstel at a kiosk near the station. David was still telling jokes. I was out of cigarettes, but feeling better as the air started to cool down. Feeling better as the drinks took hold. I talked with the other runners about saving and getting out, about going to Turkey, or Yugoslavia, or Israel. We talked like Athens wasn't a hole you kept digging and filling back up, about how much picking paid, or how much busking paid. Most of them were on their way through. But some were there forever, like David and others whose crimes you could only speculate about in the drunken boredom of waiting.

Jezz was supposed to have been on his way through, too. But now he was caught there, some bad joke for out at the bar. And I had returned to be the punchline.

When I first arrived last year Jezz had already been working for two months. He was running the train I came in on in fact, Florence to Athens—thirty hours counting break downs and stops. I had been alone since leaving the states and I had fifty dollars left.

I need work right away, I told him.

He nodded. He wore a faded black t-shirt with a picture of Lou Reed on it, and blue cut-offs. His hair was shaved in the back, it hung in his eyes and he was sweating. He smiled, lit two cigarettes and offered me one.

Where you from? he asked.

America, I told him.

I thought Americans talked like this, he said. And then he squinted and put on a fake grin and said how-dy.

No, I said. *That's how cowboys talk.*

He smiled, *And just where do cowboys come from?* he asked.

Movies, I said, looking at his face. And something shifted, opened up inside his eyes. Made room for me. Then he smiled his beautiful smile.

We stood in the aisle with our arms hanging out the window, sweating. And we talked about how a rockabilly show he had seen in London was surprisingly similar to parts of *Death on the Installment Plan,* by Ferdinand Celine, only not as funny. He began talking then and just didn't stop.

He lifted up his shirt to show me his stomach muscles. Had I ever seen such tiny tiny muscles? Had I? His stomach was thin and tight. *No,* I said. *Never.*

Punch me, he said, *go ahead. I can take a punch.* He told me his sister's birthday was a few days ago. And that he'd learned to play "This Monkey's Gone to Heaven" on the harmonica, which he said he'd play eight hours a day if he ever got sent to jail. We laughed at that one. Did I know how to play the game Tom Swifty? He'd teach me, then. *Here, here's one, for example...here's one 'I used to be a plumber, he piped!' or how 'bout 'That's my hairbrush, he bristled!'* It was an unbelievably stupid game. I said, *'I'm headed to Egypt, he said nile-istically.'*

Almost, he said, *you're getting it.* Did I want to see a trick? A disappearing trick? That's what he was best at. He pulled a coin out of his pocket....

I tried to imagine it now. I tried to force his smile on my senses to feel the hair on the back of my neck stand up. I tried to hear his jokes, but I'd heard them all before. I called upon his smell, his voice, the corner of his lip, his eyes. I called on these things for company, but they didn't exist anymore. He couldn't be counted on. Especially now.

Athens is okay, he'd said. *But you can't sleep outside, and you can't sleep in the stations. And it's not like Eastern Europe where you can live in a parking garage for a few weeks if you need to. The idea is to get to the islands. If you can make enough money in the city or picking somewhere.*

I understood him. He knew I wasn't a tourist, knew what I was. We recognized one another. He would get no commission on me. The train was full of boys holding leaflets, crowding the aisles. I thought I smelled something sweet on his breath. Then he smiled. *Can you run?* he asked.

*

Bone?

Hey. Bone.

Bone! Wake up.

Wake up, bonehead. Time to go.

I nodded and felt sneakers being jammed on my feet, and felt the blisters at my achilles tendon.

C'mon. Little Brennan, Wake up. He turned on a light.

I'm up. I'm up, I said.

Open your eyes, then.

He pulled me into a sitting position on the couch. Then he shook me and I squinted. He was wearing shorts and a gray t-shirt that said ARMY on it. And so was I. My sneakers were untied and he knelt before me tying them roughly and quickly. Then he stood and stretched. Then he did his jumping jacks. It was still dark out. The light inside shone against the empty television screen, where my brother's tiny concave reflection did its morning warm up.

Being awake was confirmed by various pains which were to be ignored.

John said, *Get it together, dogbody, get your fucking shit together or you'll be hurting for miles.*

I went to the bathroom and drank some water. The medicine cabinet was too high for me to reach so I stood on a chair to open it and get some rubber bands for my hair and white tape to put over the blisters. I brushed my teeth. My ankles hurt when I stepped down from the chair.

Alright, girl of steel. He clapped his hands. *Four feet of muscle.*

Four feet of blister, I said.

Suck it up, little fag. Let's go. Move on out. Go-go-go-go-go-go-go.

We exited the apartment and ran along the path in the housing complex, then out to First Division Drive, past the brick chapel with the white steeple, to the turn off that would lead us to the track. On the track it didn't matter if I kept up with him or not. But I still had to finish five miles before school. The air was warm and humid and the sky was growing lighter, once you started to run there was no more pain. That was the lesson in all of it, my brother said, no more pain.

*

A runner's job is to tell the most creative lies about his hotel. Every hotel was almost identical. They were all located in the red light district, none of them had bathrooms in the room, they rarely had hot water, they rarely had breakfast, and they were all very far away from the Acropolis. Summer was the best time to get robbed in these places. Cameras, passports, money. Everyone on the train had these things and many of them would be parting with them in just a few hours. My one advantage as a runner for Olympos was that it was slightly closer to the train station than the other hotels. That made a difference; made it easier to bring back tourists on late trains like the 309.

The train pulled in an hour and a half late and rusted to a stop. The windows were full of yellow light and young faces getting ready to be amazed. David swung open the door of the first passenger car, and was already selling Athens Inn before most of us had stumbled to our feet.

We boarded and walked down the aisle, and began to lie and lie. We were trying to establish some rapport with the passengers. They were all excited to be so close to Athens, and it made me feel sick and a little sorry for them. I told everyone I talked to they could sleep on our roof for five hundred drachmas, then found an empty seat and passed out. I was smacked into consciousness what seemed like seconds later.

"I told you not to sleep on the train," David said in disgust. "Wipe your mouth, we'll be there in five minutes."

We pulled into Larissis station. A crowd of well dressed tourists with bright pastel colored packs stepped down from the train looking at their maps and hotel brochures.

I paced the platform holding my leaflets above my head. Runners were screaming out their hotel names, and trying to herd tourists behind them. David and a couple of hard-ass runners had gathered a pretty big crowd.

"Maya, Olympos has how many beds?" he yelled to me.

"I don't know. Maybe fifteen tonight."

"Athens Inn can't hold this many people. Can you take these six with you?"

I nodded. "Thanks."

"Always welcome, luv." He winked and headed out leading a crowd of backpackers through the station. "I'll wake you tomorrow," he called.

I now had four Germans and two Australians to lead back to the hotel. I'd get six hundred commission plus my standard per day, so I was feeling pretty good.

"You're from Australia?"

"Yeah."

"What are you doing here? Not staying long in the city I hope?"

"No, just going to check out the Acropolis and on to the islands."

"What island are you going to?"

"Ios."

"I should have known. Buy your tickets at the port though, don't buy them in Athens."

"Okay."

"And stay the hell out of that park," I said as we rounded the corner at Diligianni. "Some Dutch guy was raped and beaten to death there last year. He was trying to sleep there," I laughed.

"No worries."

We arrived at Olympos and crowded around the reception desk in the tiny lobby.

"Dimitri," I said. "A room for four and a room for two."

"Oh, I-I-I am so sorry for tonight we h-have o-only s-singles." He grinned and shrugged, tilting his head to the side and closing his eyes.

"How much is it in marks?" asked one of the German boys.

Dimitri stammered something to him in German; they handed him their money and the Australians gave in as well. Dimitri handed me the keys, and I started up the stairs. I showed them their rooms, receiving disgusted looks in turn from six people too tired to start looking for a new hotel.

"Sweet Dreams," I told them, "bathroom's at the end of the hall. The water is usually hot by eight or nine. It's solar heating."

Then I ran downstairs to collect my money.

"Okay Dimitri, that's one-fifty for the singles."

"No no, o-one hundred p-per person."

"Singles go for one-fifty," I told him.

"Okay then, you get zero."

"The hell I do."

"You only bring six p-people, and you s-stink like liquor."

"I'd be sad if I got cheated out of my commission after running that train. I'd be really unhappy."

"So? Then y-you be s-s-sad."

His pores were enormous and his face was enormous and he shifted with great difficulty in his chair behind the reception desk. His eyes were light green and his skin was shiny and I wanted to kill him right then.

"You know David, don't you, Dimitri?"

"You are an un-un-unjust l-little girl. You th-think I have pension with this job? You think George pays me so well?"

"You do know him don't you? Just give me my money, Dimitri. It's three god damn dollars. We had other vacant rooms for them. We always have vacant rooms. What are you going to do with three dollars? Jesus, I didn't ask you to sell singles. "

"Ha. You are in no p-p-position to ask for anything. A runner he i-i-is like a beggar. You g-give him money and he dr-dr-inks with it. Money I give to m-m-my family."

"You don't have a family. You're not even married!"

"Of-of-of course I have a f-f-family. Everybody h-has family."

"Jesus Christ, Dimitri, just give me my standard commission. If I have to talk to you anymore I'll go insane. And you don't have a family. A family...what the fuck?"

He handed me two hundred drachmas, not even half of my money, without looking at me and lay one of his Dunhills on the pile of bills.

I took the money and put the cigarette in my mouth. Dimitri lit it and I walked out and down Diligianni's side streets, disgusted, looking for my friends. I would end up at Drinks Time and they would be there.

3

Waiting, I told myself. Waiting now for the black out, merciful and swift to come for me. I could detect it out there, the edges of the room growing narrower. Waiting, for there to be nothing but a fading pin point of focused vision extinguished by a black field. Waiting for sight to be replaced with sound. That barely audible high pitched hum that turns to silence, turns to nothing but the sound of blood moving relentlessly through the body.

"Maya!"

"I can't get over this place being called Drinks Time. Don't they speak English here?"

"No, they speak Greek."

"Yeah, well...."

"Maya!" I heard.

"What?" I turned around from the table and squinted through the smoke and saw no one.

"What's wrong with you?"

"Nothing," I said. "Nothing. Who's round is it? I'm dry. Hey, what's your name?

"You know me god damn name. It's Mike."

"Right, okay Mike, and what's your commission on singles?"

"I dunno, one-fifty?"

"Okay, did you get any singles?"

"Yeah."

"Okay, well would you buy me an Amstel. Okay? Cause I'm certain it's your round by now, a pint, Mike."

The bar was filled with Athens' finest illegal alien population. Drinks Time played old American movies somehow on their large screen TV, and we all went over to spend the night in a kind of stupefied nostalgia. Everyone watched American movies, no matter where they were from. I could never stand television.

Well-dressed Arab men stood at the bar. They were involved in some kind of constant exchange of glances and items. Standing with perfect posture, but with their shoulders slightly curved beneath loose long-sleeved silk shirts. Bracelets on wide wrists. There was an easiness about them that could vanish at any moment. When Jezz lived in Athens he had smoked their Dunhills, their Benson and Hedges, their Marlboros. And he had exchanged our names, our addresses and identities for three thousand dollars, a beer and a shot. The problem was you could only lose your own passports once. After that you had to sell the "lost" documents of others. After that there was a certain amount of stamina involved. And the ability to take a beating every once and a while. Jezz did it for some reason of his own. Because it was real, he said. And the money lay around our room getting lost or stolen or given away, paying for round after round. I don't know what happened to it.

Selling was all a diversion of some kind. It was something that kept you in motion. In fear. Something that allowed you to tune in to the beautiful silent gestures all around. That forced you to. It allowed you to become a scholar in the field of pupil dilation, sweat, facial tics, words, gestures, expressions. And then if you were lucky, actual feelings. Panic, elation, the sudden realization that everything is alive and you can watch it rise and fall. It can swallow you or you can ride it out. Selling for Jezz wasn't about money. It was about keeping his blood the correct temperature so that he didn't fall asleep and die.

I couldn't figure out what film was playing. It was hard to pay attention. There had been landscape shots so far. Aerial views of cliffs, beaches, oceans, forests, highways, buildings, factories. All beautifully abandoned. I turned my pint upside down and let the last few drops of beer fall on to my tongue, while I waited for the next round.

Maya! I heard again.

"What?" I whispered.

Maya, we're in the money babe.

"Sh," I said without looking, "Quit with that American accent," I said, though I had always liked it.

A solitary figure on the TV was digging a hole, not too deep, with gently sloping sides. He climbed out and put the shovel down, uncorked a bottle of wine and poured it all into the hole. That'll bring them to the surface, he muttered.

Maya, I've got one hundred and fifty thousand drachmas.

I looked up at him. And smiled. Brilliant! He actually looked alive, his best trick ever. My lungs opened up and my vision came into sharp focus. "Oh my God, Jezz," I laughed. "How did you get it?"

Six German, four British, and an American. And none of 'em expire for another five years.

He grinned wide at me. His hair was full of sweat and looked almost brown. He was wearing a black t-shirt and had a beaten copy of the *Viking Portable Library of William Blake* folded up and stuffed into the back pocket of his cut-offs. His feet were bare, long, thin and dirty. He was thirsty. And he had come up to drink from the hole on the television. He had come up, like a thirsty specter, to tell me what had happened.

"Oh, God, we're going to have to leave. I can't believe you just.... How can you? I've... We've got to leave now. We can go to Prague. We can live for years on that."

Yeah. That's exactly what I thought, he said, wiping the sweat off his face with his hands. *But first we'll have to buy rounds.* He smiled and wiped his face again on the front of his shirt.

"Oi. Here's yer Amstel. Maya...? Here's yer Amstel," Mike sang, waving the pint back and forth in front of my face.

"We can leave tomorrow," I said and watched as Jezz's tongue caught the sweat running down his upper lip.

"Are you going somewhere?" Mike interrupted.

"Yeah," I said taking the beer.

"You just got here."

"No." I turned to him, "I have been waiting here for a very long time. I've just been waiting around for months. All we fucking do here is wait. There is nothing else!" I laughed. "Nothing!" I laughed some more. "Absolutely nothing!"

"God, she's fucked," Mike said to some vaguely familiar people at the table. Their faces were inscrutable. "How many's she had?" he asked. But he was murmuring now, he was ambient sound.

"I know man, last year it was Buddy Holly, now it sounds like she's actually talking to Jezz for fucks sake." There was laughter. Someone spit part of their drink and it fanned out in droplets of light. Perfectly round, silver, slow motion.

"But leave her alone, div'nee even kid her," someone said. "That Irish guy'll kill you, lit'rally kill you if you fuck with her. She walks around like nothing can fuckin' hurt her."

Jezz put his hand around my bottle of Amstel and steam rose from it. He let his head roll back and his mouth fell open slightly. I took the beer out of his hand and drank and he straightened up and watched me for a while. I could look into his eyes and they were only slightly sunken, but still all blue and shiny deep black. Warm and cold, earth and space. They were still my home.

"She's was like that before," said Mike's voice. "They all three were.

Y'shoulda seen them together. Th'bastards. It has nothing to do with David. Who's round?"

Buy rounds, and then we'll go up to the Acropolis, Jezz said to me, taking out his book and fanning himself with it. Never breaking his gaze. Never looking at the blurry room.

"It's three a.m., we can't get through the gate."

Gosh, it's motherfucking hot in here, he said. *Isn't it, darlin'?*

"We can leave though right? We'll get a deck class to Rhodes to start, or maybe back to Brindisi. Who says you can't get out?" I said smiling at him.

He kneeled before my place at the table and licked the wet ring left by my beer. I watched him. I could smell his hair, waxy and unwashed. Sweat ran down the sides of his face, down his neck and into his shirt. He was so much prettier now. The only thing that had had any power over him was gone. And he was radiant! weightless! I liked him more than ever. We'd find our man Jack Rollock and get out of Athens for a little while. The three of us, like old times. But just the three of us this time. No interruptions. No Passports.

I took a long drink and then held the bottle to his burning cheek. *I thought they said you won't get out, Princess.* He put his hand over mine and smirked cruelly, *Run for your money and you won't get out.*

*

I woke up back at Olympos, too early, with a dry mouth and covered with sweat. I pulled my bag over to the side of the bed and got out another pack of Camels, leaned there for a while waiting to feel sick. I would be sick soon. I would vomit soon, as I did now every morning. I reached slowly for my cigarettes. When this carton's empty, I thought, I will have saved fifteen dollars. Maybe I could go to the islands before I have to start smoking Navys. I couldn't afford to keep smoking. I had to save.

I sat and smoked and counted my money. The waves of nausea came and went. I wanted them to settle so I could get up and start moving again. I had to get going, and my stomach was slowing me down. The lack of money was impressive considering how much I had managed to spend just doing nothing. And how much I'd made selling my original passport.

I remembered that day at the consulate. The day I got a new one issued. I was the last of the three of us to do it.

It had been a worthwhile hassle, and made us fifteen hundred dollars. I'd filled out the paperwork, but I'd no other identification.

Z5530900 I wrote down, sitting at a little desk to the right of the window in the marble and tile hall of the American consulate. That had been my passport number. Then Name: Brennan, Maya Kathleen. Sex: I got an 'F' in that category. Birthplace: NY, USA. Birthdate: 2/10/73. Nationality: 'you put 'drunkard' down for that one right?!'

I slid the form and the square photo booth picture of my face beneath the glass that separated me from the bald, suited official. He took it, went away and then came back with questions.

Where did I go to school?

Where had I been staying?

How much money did I have?

Who were my parents?

Where were they?

I looked bad—did I need some clothes or lunch maybe?

No?

Name of the hotel again?

I'd been traveling for how long?

Sure I wasn't working here? Begging here?

Did I know the same drug laws were enforced in Greece as in the U.S.? Stricter, in fact?

No money? No passport? No return ticket? No ID?

No. Passport. I'd have to wait in this room...I'd have to be interviewed by...

I live with my brother, I told him. He's Airborne Special Forces retired. He goes to Cornell University on the GI bill. I watched his face relax as he recast me in his mind. I'll be going home at the end of the summer, I said, standing straight and looking into his face. He's seen to it.

He set the forms down and looked at me. Roughing it, eh?

I smiled. Yeah. Roughing it.

Trust...amused will to assist. I watched myself in his face, move fluidly from a desperate loser with suspect motivations, to 'cute.' To 'spunky tomboy.' Watched myself move from a check list of details in a consulate training film called 'how to identify a drug trafficker' to a cameo role in a film about an orphan in which Shirley Temple salutes. The reverence on his face was hilarious. I had to pause with my lines—it looked like we might have to take a curtain call right there, so genius was his comic parody. That solemn understanding he had with himself. The will to support a good kid down on her luck. I mean after all I was American. We were American. He'd support my God given right to a passport, for the U.S.A., and for the sacrifices my brother'd made. My brother Sergent-First-Class-Special-Forces-Airborne. It took eight seconds. And another half an hour to get the document.

Okay Maya, you're all set.

Thank you for squaring me away, sir.

He smiled at that. It's issued for a year—get your brother to send us a copy of your birth certificate and we can extend it for you right away for ten—or you can just take care of it when you get home.

I sure will, sir. Thank you, now.

And I was Maya Brennan again, a few years older in the new photograph. And it might have all been fine if we'd have stopped there.

I stubbed out my cigarette. My stomach had begun to settle. The room was bright and hot and I had no idea what time it was. I got up and opened the balcony door for some air. It was like opening an oven. There was no guessing the time by the amount of traffic. Diligianni Street always had heavy traffic, night and day. I stood on the balcony squinting at the train station's clock in the distance, but couldn't make out its face. I leaned on the railing and breathed in the hot haze. In Athens hundreds of people became sick every summer from breathing, so a lot of them just stopped doing it altogether. Last summer seven hundred people were hospitalized. I always thought breathing in midday was like getting burned. The air was like hot dirty steel being pressed to the inside of your body. I took a deep breath, maybe I could cauterize my belly with this air.

I closed up the balcony and walked over to the sink and washed my hair with a bar of soap. I rinsed the sweat off my body and stood dripping in the hot morning air and smoking with a towel on my head.

Trying not to look at how empty the room was.

I listened to the cars race by outside. Then I tried to cry for a few minutes. I squinted, took a deep breath and held it. Then I made a kind of high pitched sound in my throat. I even said "Jezz" out loud, thinking that would help. But it was no use.

I pulled on a pair of cut-offs and a t-shirt and a pair of jungle boots my brother had given me before I left the states. They were so worn-in you could wear them without socks. They made me feel okay. People feel shitty if they just stay still, sitting around with a stomach ache in a hotel room. Even a few minutes too long could mess you up.

I did a few jumping jacks and thought in concrete terms about the room. And how it didn't signify anything really. It had never been beautiful. Beautiful was an optical illusion. I put money in my boot and walked across the bare concrete to room thirty-two. If there were other runners in the hotel that's where they'd be. And they might know something about Jack.

The only rooms on the top floor belonged to runners. The rest of the floor was missing. There was an archway that lead out on to the crumbling remains of a lower roof, and that was it. The other levels of the hotel had nine rooms and a bathroom at the end of the corridor. But on this level it looked as though a small bomb had gone off, taking more than half of the floor with it. And they'd just slapped tile on the exposed lower level, leaving Olympos unfinished and waiting to fall apart. I don't know what the story was with that floor—maybe it had been constructed badly and had crumbled. It looked good in a way, and was only really a problem if it rained. We got to live up there for free so what did it matter?

I knocked on the door and after some time Nigel opened it.

"You still alive?" He stood in his boxers with a glazed look in his eyes. "It's eight in the bloody mornin."

"Yeah? Well, how are you man? I haven't seen you in months!"

"You saw me last night," he said.

He had short, straight, mousy hair and brown eyes. He dressed more like tourist than a runner. He never talked about leaving or traveling. He never complained about running. He spent his free time and all of his money eating in restaurants and drinking in Drinks Time.

We stared at each other for a while. Finally he said, "For fucks sake." And shut the door.

I ran down stairs after walking around the roof for a while, and swung around the banister to stand in front of Sterious who was holding his tiny coffee cup.

"I need train fare," I told him. "And I need to know what train I'm running."

"Maya again is on the 309," he said.

"The 309 is a zoo."

"Yes, there are many people on this train. We need a girl on it."

"And that bastard Dimitri is running the desk at night. You know that right? He didn't give me my commission."

"Dimitri!" He spat.

"He can speak a lot of languages though, huh?"

"If you can stand to listen. He was not in the Navy. Oh no.

"Of course not, look at him."

"He's of a rich man's son," said Sterious. "How else he could learn to talk so much?"

"How did you learn languages?"

"The Navy. Hold out your hand." He gave me a handful of pistachios from his sweater pocket. Even in mid summer he wore cardigans, like some strange caricature of an old man. The skin on his hands was soft and his knuckles were large and misshapen. "Okay," he continued, "what did you do in Palestine?"

"I picked fruit, Sterious. Remember?"

"Did you get pregnant?"

I said nothing.

"Don't make this face to me. You look fatter. And it is against God to marry a Jew."

"I didn't marry anyone while I was there."

"You want coffee?"

He turned on the electric pot that stood on the floor near his chair, and spooned some black powder into a tiny cup that matched his own.

"You like Greek?"

"Mm-hm," I said eating another pistachio.

"Yes. Dimitri is some kind of stupid man. He is a bad man. Do you know what is a moron? Dimitri. He is what is a moron."

"Mm-hm."

It seemed like it would be nice to sit for a while on the cold tile of the steps and talk with him. Maybe watch people go by, maybe keep him company. But I knew I couldn't make myself do it. I had to get moving.

I drank my shot of sweet coffee and spit some grounds back in the cup. "I need train fare."

"Yes-yes-yes." He unlocked a drawer in the reception desk and gave me two hundred drachmas in coins. "Don't miss the train."

I handed him the cup and pocketed the change and the rest of the nuts, and I turned to go just as David was walking in. He looked very clean and his head was newly shaved, shiny, even in the dim reception office. He gave me a toothy grin.

"I was coming to wake you up," he said.

"Too late."

He nodded, smiled. "You do much better without your mates," he said. "Mike said you passed out in Drinks Time. Talking to your imaginary friends, yeah?"

I shrugged.

"Let's go to the Plaka," he said.

"I have to be on the 309," I told him.

"Me as well," he said, putting his arm around my shoulder and leading me down the steps. "Jesus is on the cross, Maya, and he calls to Peter. 'Peter' he says, 'Peter...' 'Yes my lord?' 'I can see your house from here.'" He laughed and slapped me on the back. Then he squeezed me to his side. It felt nice to walk with him in the morning.

We headed up Diligianni towards the center of town. Small cars rushed by us on the dirty street as we passed vacant and destroyed buildings, kiosks, and small bakeries. After several blocks more, shops began to appear, fruit vendors, bigger official looking buildings; then souvenir shops and larger kiosks that sold pornography, knives, fake guns, and ice cream. People began filling the streets and squares as we got closer to the Plaka. Voices rose above the noise of traffic, and everywhere the smell of lamb cooking mixed with the other odors of the street and followed us. We stopped at a vendor and bought a paper cone filled with cherries.

"We ought to go get a souvlaki," he said watching me eat.

"Yeah."

"I love this city," he said, unbuttoning his jean jacket and the first few buttons of his shirt "Where else in the world can you eat so well so cheap?" He was looking straight ahead.

"Nowhere."

"Never rains, never snows."

"It rains here all autumn," I said.

"But it never snows."

"It rains here all winter too."

"And the Acropolis..." he went on.

I laughed. "I don't care what you say, runner, I'm not staying in your hotel."

We wound our way past the National Museum and the First Bank of Greece and headed for the flea market near Monasturaki. Above all of that was the Acropolis, supernal and white with green cranes towering above the temples. Without a hint of irony, the ruins were being restored. I wished they'd leave the cranes there forever, to rust among the columns.

The concrete under our feet was replaced by brown brick, and the buildings became smaller and huddled together. Finally the cars disappeared. Merchants lined the streets smoking and standing in front of their shops. Sandal makers called to me as we walked by, trying to entice me into their underground workshops.

"You look like a boy in boots," they called. "Its no good to look like boys."

The sandals were beautiful, too. The long laces wound up your legs like in the classical drawings of Greek soldiers; brown and black leather, sewed by hand. When they were new you skidded across all the smooth streets and fell, until they were old and dirty enough to carry you right. David used to say that they weren't good until you had pissed on them and worn them after, to mold them to your feet.

We passed weavers and guitar makers and potters and souvenir shops filled with key chains and little statues of satyrs with their comic and devious hard-ons. The alleyways were narrow and cool and everything resonated with sounds.

I stopped to light a cigarette and we walked another few blocks through the alleys into the open square to Argos. It was a little basement restaurant that didn't send hosts out into the street to nag you into stopping and they had Greek regulars which was nice to see.

We went in and took a table under a small window. Old men were crouched at the bar, drinking little cups of coffee and playing cards. The place smelled of lamb and oregano and cinnamon. A waiter came over and asked us what we wanted in American English.

"Water," said David.

"And Amstel," I said.

We ordered two souvlaki.

"This is what I missed," I said in anticipation of the meal. "I missed the feta and the meat."

"Its nice there's no runners here." He smiled at me with his eyes.

"Too far uptown. They'll never crawl up here this early."

"Yeah," he said, "and they play Greek music, that ought to keep them away."

"Maybe if they didn't play it at the station all day you could stand it."

"You can't stand a thing and that's a fact."

"Yeah."

"Why did you leave Israel?" he asked.

"I couldn't stand the music."

"No, truly, should I have to go there?"

"Why do you always assume that I am trying to get away from something? I wanted to be there; then I wanted to come back and travel with Jezz. My timing was off, that's all."

He laughed hard. "Yeah, your timing.... But why did you stay so long away?"

"It was just a few months."

The waiter put a plate of tzatziki and pita bread on our table, and I began to eat.

"You didn't miss him or you'd a been back sooner, am I right? Ah, but, how could you miss him though after alla his bollocks? You know what I mean." I knew what he meant, but he didn't. What Jezz did to feel alright didn't bother me, it was his inability to keep moving that did. The words "trafficker" and "runner" were misused as they applied to him. Jezz was an idler.

David shook his head in disappointment. And it wasn't one of those squad leader gestures, those calculated gestures that are offered up as cues. It was sincere. We'd kept the passports secret from him, and it seemed that he still didn't know anything about it. His main troubles with Jezz had been his drinking, and sarcasm, and the class of his accent. But still they were close. They had always been close.

"Well, I waited with him to see if y'missed him enough t'come back." David said.

"I had no money to come back initially," I told him. "I spent my last thirty bucks on the deck class. Then I got stuck on a kibbutz pulling in a dollar a day. The cigarettes were free there. Finally, I got a job picking, you know, which was a lucky break. The work was good, great actually, it was hard. You had to use your body, and the trees were beautiful, David. They were just beautiful. They were..."

"Ah, don't start."

"Well, anyway. It was relaxing like that. But I didn't like much else about being there. Like you said, there's nowhere as good as Greece. And anyway I didn't like their soldiers."

I sopped up the last of the tzatziki with some pita bread and shoved it in my mouth.

"Hearts and minds," David said.

"Exactly. Who needs it?"

"Don't talk with your mouth full, little miss."

Our souvlaki came, big chunks of lamb on skewers. We ate quickly in silence. Afterwards I got another beer and smoked leaning back in my chair. David drank his water, and surveyed the room. He was almost awkward when he was alone. When it was just him and you. He needed a crowd to play to, or maybe just to be in. He must have missed all three of us. It must have been hard without us.

Last year he would come every morning at the same time to wake Jezz and Jack and me. He brought us chocolate milk, the kind that comes in small plastic bags with a pointed straw. And sometimes he brought us orange juice and cookies and we'd sit in our shorts on the cold tile and have breakfast together. I don't know why it was us. Maybe some weakness he could see, maybe it was our senses of humor. But it was hard to shake his friendship once we had it.

Me being Irish was some big thing for him, Irish and American and raised like I was, and Jack being black, and Jezz being Jezz. David had singled us out for divine surveillance, and we were protected. We did impressions of him when he was out of earshot. Jezz was good with the accent, but I could do his look better than anyone. None of us have loyalties, he'd said, look at us, we're Spartans here. We're Spartan soldiers.... No loyalties. None.

He wanted us to function as a group, and we did. But sometimes we couldn't be found. And sometimes one of us was too drunk to run. Afternoons were ours, and late nights. But mornings and runs belonged to David. And it wasn't too much for him to ask. We were his squad. He said we were his squad. But whatever it was we were being built up to carry out we never did. Unless it was drink and fuck, and he never did that with us. He did other things with us instead.

You're not scared, David had said. You're not stupid. None of you are stupid. So I'm a little confused by your behavior. And I think you're a little confused as well. You are. I can see it. You just need to understand.

He had broken Jezz's arm in two places and then wouldn't let him go to the hospital. Wouldn't let me and Jack leave the room.

You feel that? he had asked Now, do you want more Metaxa or do you need more Metaxa?

Jezz had shuddered, taken deep breaths through his teeth. He looked like he might be sick. And it was his own fault. He had never learned how to just listen and not be afraid. If you just listen, things unfold. And most of the time nothing happened. Most of the time it was okay. Nothing David did scared me, because I trusted him. I knew how to take instructions, or look like I knew. I was versed in this kind of thing. Watching without seeing. And I knew when to leave, when to cut and run.

Do you know the difference between want and need? David leered at him. See, 'cause now you actually need a drink. Jezz was incredibly pale. Maya, Jezz needs a drink. Go get him some more Metaxa, luv. He held out a few bills to me. But I could see Jezz didn't want me to leave. I stood looking at him for a moment.

I said go. get. Jezz. some more. Bloody Metaxa. Before I Break. His. Other. Arm.

I looked up at David now. Looked at his square face. It's important to limit your time together, though, friend or not. Trust or not. It's important to know how to do these things.

"Hearts and minds," David said again. "I never gave my heart and mind,"

"What?" I asked as though I hadn't heard him.

"Sold it; sold it long ago."

This was again the unpleasant beginning of details I didn't need, and I looked for ways to twist what he was about to say; a sentence that would begin with 'Angola was a mess' and was coming any minute. You never actually got to hear the Angola story—he never actually told it, but there were expected responses.

"You believed in what you were doing," I said to him putting out my cigarette.

He laughed, "Angola was a mess though. That fucked me. It really did. I've never made so much money in my life. Bloody American's. Argentina, Brazil, they didn't fuck me like Angola. Painless. Brazil, that was just a training team. Ah, It was hilarious, though. In Brazil they brought in doctors, we didn't have to do that much. They had this communist woman in the prison, where we were stationed. And they removed her lips and teeth and they implanted the incisors of a dog in her mouth. Then they sealed her mouth. Sealed it up real smooth, plastic surgery like, and let her go so she could be an example. You'd think twice after seeing that. Imagine her comrades' faces when they had her mouth opened and they found the doggy teeth, saw the thoroughness. Just the thoroughness." He laughed and barked like a dog.

We left money on the table and walked into the square.

He took my hand instinctively as we crossed the street.

4

Jezz left nothing. His clothes had been taken by other runners. His glasses and even his books were gone. He was gone. I had a small silver hoop earring that was a match to one he wore, but I was sure his parents had taken it out before burying him. I was having a hard time believing that he was dead, that he'd actually died from drinking. He was too good at it. If I were to retrace his steps, I thought, redrink his drinks, it would take me several years to get where he did. To get jaundiced like that. To get that sick, even in my current state. There was no way.

I sipped my pint without picking it up off the table. Looked out the window at the heat rising from a car that idled by the curb, rested my hand against my belly.

I remembered lying in bed with Jezz, leaning against the wall drinking beer and reading a Viz comic. It was a great issue. Johnny Fartpants was trying to get a job. Some character with a black mohawk had got his dick caught in his zipper! And then cut himself shaving! And then accidentally ate glass! And there was an article on the queen presenting an award to an African tribal leader whose name was Bumfuk. She called him "Mr. Bumfuk." Which is what Jezz called Jack for the next month. Hello Mr. Bumfuk, and will you be joining us this evening Mr. Bumfuk? I am breaking off diplomatic relations with you Mr. Bumfuk, unless you purchase another carton of fags...Mr. fucking Bumfuk. Manchester fag sponger. Hey, it's your turn to purchase the fags, Jack. Jack Luv?

I remembered us lying on the roof. It was a night too hot to sleep. And we drew maps in the dust; next Cypress, next Morocco, next Thailand. Next time. The pleasure of places, of motion. I wanted to be alone with him then, while we drank together, but it didn't matter. I wanted to be alone with him and so did Jack.

Thinking about it made me sick again. All of it tightened in my chest. Gave me a fucking nose bleed. The weight of his body still pressed against me like a ghost limb. When I looked up across the table I expected to see him. I expected to see him walking past the window of the bar, or down the corridor of a train. Every place in the city resonated with his absence. He'd made me a wraith in the world of his death; a vast empty square, lined with the long shadows of those who aren't there. He left me to remember him better than I ever knew him. And I called to him now with memory.

The memory of waking up on the balcony from the sound of traffic and the sudden shock of sobriety, and letting myself into the room through the glass doors. Jack was sleeping by the balcony in his boxers with a pillow over his head, his hands locked over it, his long flat feet hanging off the edge of the bed.

Jezz was lying unconscious on the cot across from the sink. His bed was ringed with his possessions. Bottles, cigarettes, clothes, books and comic books. His pale skin shone in the gray light like a body floating just below the surface of water. I remember I was very awake, and sat on the cold tile with my back against his cot, smoking his cigarettes and trying to read one of his books by the light of the burning ash. I read the same lines over and over again until my eyes hurt. And he breathed heavily behind me. I turned and held the cigarette very close to him so I could see him in the red glow. Smelled his hair, put my face against his. I got in bed with him and lay on my back looking at our bodies side by side. Ribs and hip bones and small pale bellies. And if he'd open his eyes they'd look exactly like mine, only blue. Only redder. I closed my eyes and held his sleeping hand. I would fall asleep like this. Waiting beside the paler blonder boy body that was now vicariously mine. And for a while it was alright. For a while it was all internal time, slack time, autonomy. An unspoken assention that we had come from the same country, to the same country. That we had reached the right place separately and found each other. And it was beautiful there. Bright overcast haze, darkness and clouds, traffic and silence, the smell of diesel and baking bread. And all around the low, white, post-war architecture of seventies movies and Japanese animation and dead intellectuals. An internal landscape turned inside out.

Now I had nothing and there was nothing left of him. I rubbed the back of my hand across my top lip to catch the blood then held my head back. In less than a year he had gone from bad to dead. Why hadn't it happened to someone else?

"Genetic," Nigel mumbled, picking up a bar napkin and pushing it towards my nose. "He probably had some predisposition to dying young."

"He was nineteen, Nige, dying young means before thirty." I sat up and let the blood drip into the napkin, set down my empty pint and looked at him.

"Hmmm."

"Did he say he was expecting his folks?"

"Last I talked to him," Nigel said, still looking at the TV, "he was doing this magic trick where you put a fifty drachma piece in your ear and take it out from under your tongue."

"Was he good at it?"

"No. What do you think? He ever do a trick you couldn't figure out? You could hear him trying to talk with the coin in his mouth before he even started. Then he stayed in bed for a week or so, all paranoid. He was passed out a lot. I came home from a run one day and he was gone. Just like that. Was a day or so before it got really hot."

"How did his parents figure to come and get him?"

"He was fucked."

"No, I mean how did they know that?"

"I don't know. Does it matter?"

"Someone had to have called them."

"Probably."

"Where's Jack Rollock?"

"Who?"

"Black Jack."

"Flak Jacket? He's gone too. Left after a run; didn't show up at Drinks Time. Your round," he said, staring at his empty mug.

I went up to the bar and bought two more pints, threw away the wet red bar napkin. A movie called *The Omega Man* was playing on the big screen. Charleton Heston was running from some book burning mutants.

"That's what's going to happen," said Nigel pointing at the TV. "You Americans are going to nuke everything, and we'll destroy all that's left. All that reminds us of culture."

Nigel was an idiot. He once told me that in the space of a month he had taken fifty hits of acid, and I was beginning to believe it. 'I was blinded' he had told me, 'and I finally knew that there was only really darkness, and there would always be darkness. It's all black and you say at last I know.'

And now I was watching him watch a movie, in which Charleton Heston was watching a movie.

I said, "where do you think Jack's gone?"

"Away. Look, they can just go into those stores and take what they want."

"Mm hm."

"Yeah man, I had a dream about this movie once."

I finished my beer. "Your round, Nige."

He got up and bought two more.

"We have to be on the 309 in four hours," he said, handing me my beer. "After the train you should come to Paradise. People are going to Paradise."

"To do what?"

"Drink."

"Maybe."

"Go. There's fuck all to do anyway. Look at that girl's afro. She ends up doing Charleton Heston in the end."

"Where do you think Jack's gone?"

"Away."

"What about...listen, what about...."

"Shut up," he said again in an exasperated whisper like he was talking to himself.

We watched the rest of the movie. The bar was dead except for us and some broken down middle-aged man sitting near the door. He spoke to the bartender in a horrible Mancunian accent, he wore too much cologne and appeared to be very drunk. The afternoons were desolate.

"Maya, your round." Nigel nudged me with his empty mug.

"No man, I've got to take a nap like the rest of the city. Wake me for the train."

He nodded, staring at the credits.

*

Ready? he leaned his head through the doorway and smiled. *You got your stuff, bone? Got your books? Got your smokes?* He walked into my room and just stood there. There were just two more boxes of books to load up. He tapped the heel of his boot on the toe of his other boot. *Ready, Bone?*

Yeah. I grabbed a carton of cigarettes off the empty bookcase.

There had been a lot of frozen food and oatmeal and stuff like that left in the house. But I broke down when the electricity got cut-off.

I panicked instead of trying to solve it myself. And he came in his olive green t-shirt and his faded Levis. He'd already registered me for sixth grade on base. It was August. Just before he was about to turn twenty-one. So he said things worked out perfectly. He said it was providence. He said things were squared away.

He put the duffel bag over his shoulder and we walked through the house. The screen door swung shut behind us on its spring.

We got a real nice place at Benning. You'll drive in to base with me in the mornings and I'll drop you off at the school. And you can take the bus back to Highgate in the afternoon and I'll be home around seven every night. We're squared away, you and me. Right? Once we find a place to put all your books, huh? He laughed, then looked serious again. *You've got no disadvantage. Hear me? You're already the smartest kid on base and we're not even on base yet. Hey, you listening to me?*

In the car he talked about when he got caught in a tree and had to cut his chute away, and when he had landed on a farmers house. I pictured these things as if they had happened in our back yard. As if he were caught in our pine tree. I couldn't picture Italy or Georgia, or Belgium. He talked about our old dog. How when he was my age he had heard her heart beating with a toy stethoscope. He could hear her heart missing a beat. I smoked and tried to read while he drove and talked. I was still wearing my pajamas and the gummy shoes with daisies on them. I wanted to keep reading because if I had to go back to school I wouldn't have any more time. Since I'd been alone I had managed to read all of my books and about a quarter of the books my parents had left in the house. My books were easy, a lot of them still had pictures in them.

When my parents' books became dull I would go to the library. There was a writer named Franz Kafka who wrote short things that were as good as, if not better than, my mythology books. And another writer, Ferdinand Celine, who wrote with no chapters. He put three dots in between different ideas he had, so that the book would go fast. And it did. His books raced. They were funny. Most of the books I was bringing with me I had checked out of the library and would never return.

My brother bummed a smoke and turned on the radio. It was nice driving in the car. The sun was shining. We crossed over the state line and he looked over at me and raised his eyebrows and smiled. He took a deep breath and let it out.

After a while he said, *Why did you wait so long to call me?*

I shrugged and looked out the window.

He shook his head. *How long has she been gone?*

I shrugged. *I don't know.*

Yeah?! He threw the cigarette out the window, hit the steering wheel with the side of his fist. Then he grabbed my cigarette and threw it out the window too. *Don't. Smoke. Jesus! What ten-year-old smokes?*

I'm eleven.

Well you look like you're about six. You do not smoke anymore do you hear me? Jesus Christ, Bonehead, what the fuck is wrong with you? How long have you been in that house alone? Why didn't you call me? Why didn't you call someone? Why didn't you tell someone at school? Huh? Maya. Answer me Maya.

*

"Maya?" Nigel's voice shook me and then his hand. "Fuckin zombie," he mumbled. "Let's go, I want to get some cigarettes before the train."

I sat up and ran my hands over my sweaty hair, and got two packs of Camels out of my bag. "Here," I said, tossing him a pack. Then I ran downstairs and threw up. I barely made it to the bathroom. After the jumping jacks this morning I thought I was already over it. But the heat and the cigarettes must have gotten to me. It was a weird sickness. So sudden and uncontrollable and then completely gone. Wake up. Vomit. Evidence—more evidence of an irony that was just too complete....

Ten minutes later, we walked down to the lobby together, grabbed our leaflets from Dimitri, and cut across the park to Larissis. The park was filled with gnarled and unkempt shrubs and littered with used condoms and ouzo bottles. The ouzo bottles made me shudder.

"Run for your money," Nigel said as we approached the entrance.

5

Runners were sitting on the ground on the platform with their backs against the station wall. The people from Athens Connection and Luzani, taller, wider, and more sober than the rest of us, sat apart on benches. They carried binders with actual photographs of their rooms, bars, and dining areas. They carried timetables for boats and trains, so they could talk to the tourists about their itineraries. These runners didn't smile at anyone who didn't mean commission. They didn't raise their voices. They were there to fill their hotel and get paid, these true believers. The funny part was they got paid only as well as we did. They were professional runners. David was a professional runner—posing as a professional runner—but he ran for Athens Inn in our part of town and we respected him.

Several new faces were among the crowd I knew, and there was a real party atmosphere, a bond between the runners of the Diligianni area. They were actually anticipating the train as something fun to do.

I leaned against the wall and listened to people talk. Listened to them ask one another 'where you from?' Tonight I would really work the train, I told myself. I would really fill the hotel. I'd get ahead so I could save a little. Spend only what I had to on rounds, and then leave. I had no reason to stay now. And there was no way I'd stay three months just for Sterious, good as he was. Three months would be too late. Any amount of time now was too late.

"What's that you're humming?" asked an American accent.

A dark haired boy was sitting against the wall beside me, clutching his leaflets and tapping them nervously against his knee. He was smiling up at me. He was clean, wore new sneakers and had a watch. He didn't look like he'd been away from home for too long.

I didn't know if I had been humming or not, so I ignored his question and asked him where he was from.

"Binghamton, New York, U.S.A.," he said. "It's near..."

"I know Binghamton."

"Really?" He smiled and his teeth were unnaturally straight. "I'm running for Annabells. Small world. When were you in the states?"

"From my birth until I left. I lived in Central New York when I was a kid, and then again just before traveling. How long have you been out?"

"For close to a year," he said. "I've been at the University of Perugia for nine months."

"Christ man, how did you end up here?"

"I started to run out of money; figured this was a good place to be broke."

I nodded. "But Perugia is nice and small," I said. "You can sleep outside there. You don't need too much."

He stood up. "Yeah, it was amazing there," he said. I really could live there. Seriously. "He looked into my face, making me want to avert my eyes. "The food, man, and the people and my god, It's just fucking amazing. I really did love it. I was a little let down by Athens; but at least I'm making money instead of spending it, you know? I haven't gotten to the Acropolis yet. Have you been? Have you been to the Islands?"

"Yes. I like them."

He had sharp features. He looked closely at my face as he spoke to me. And then looked away when he described things. He talked with his hands.

"My name's Danny," he said.

"That's David," I said pointing through the crowd at him. "He's the person you want to talk to about any travel plans, David. And he's funny as hell, he's been everywhere." We watched him walk into the station. "He's good," I heard myself say. "He's good."

"What's your name?" he asked me.

"Killer," I said.

"Oh yeah? What's your real name?"

"Betty."

"Really?"

Some taxi drivers walked on to the platform from the back gate and it grew quiet.

"Who are they?" Danny asked.

"Drivers. They show up here and mess with people every few weeks. We don't even know what the fuck they're saying. They think they'd get more people riding with them to hotels uptown if we weren't here. Which is completely true, we take their business. But if they were smart they'd rat out the hotels for employing aliens. Instead of coming here and pushing people around." I dropped my cigarette on the platform and stepped on it.

A driver named Spero walked up the platform, staring down at the wall lined with runners. He was a huge man with hips as wide as his shoulders. He wore a driver's cap and a short sleeved polo shirt. The other drivers stood in a group by the back gate, watching.

Spero stopped in front of Tom, a South African boy, who ran for San Remo and smoked hashish all day. Tom looked straight up at him with no expression, and everyone was silent for a long time.

"I am the Greek king of box!" the driver bellowed holding his fists in a boxer's pose. Still no one dared to speak.

Tom's eyes got wide and his mouth twitched and then he burst out in a fit of laughter, holding his stomach and leaning on the bench next to him. We all joined him, laughing and claiming to be the kings of box. I watched Spero as he tried to decide whether he should let it come off as a joke or really fuck with us, his smile vanishing and reappearing as he envisioned himself alternately a wit or an ass; his eyes trying to read the crowd of dirty drunken foreigners; his fists still raised.

Then Tom did something insane. He stood up in front of the Greek king of box, and taking a fighter's stance, he shouted, "pusti malaka."

The drivers at the entrance turned quickly in unison, just as Spero boxed him in the jaw, sending his head directly into the brick wall of the station house. It bounced forward. His hands flew out, instinctively trying to break whatever fall might be coming, but he lost consciousness and slid to the platform, mouth bleeding.

A cry went up from the runners, and someone began screaming for the station cop who would never show up.

"Why did he do that?" Danny yelled in my ear.

"The kid said something like 'suck my dick, faggot' to him."

The other drivers moved in on the crowd, swinging. The big boys from Luzani and Athens Connection had disappeared.

Tom's friends had dragged him into the station and tucked him behind a baggage cart, leaving him there to return to the fight. I stayed where I was, hoping I would go unnoticed crouching behind a bench. I couldn't see down the platform, and I couldn't hear anything but shouting. Danny had vanished into the mass of limbs that had taken over the station. I pulled out a cigarette and smoked it lying low. This would be the first time I watched a fight with the drivers and didn't have to see Jezz get the fuck beat out of him. I stared into the sea of rushing legs and fists, and knew there was no crawling around the corner into the station without being spotted. I sat there cross-legged, protected by the bench, smoking.

More drivers had come onto the platform, or maybe it was just that a lot of runners were down, and a lot had wisely run as soon as they heard Tom's head hit brick.

Directly in front of me a driver grabbed a kid I didn't know. He had been sitting near Danny, and must have just arrived in the past few days. The driver had him by the hair and was pulling his head back, biting him on the face. He was screaming, his eyes straining, the whites bulging like a horse's as he looked from side to side, trying to somehow disassociate. I could see he wasn't doing it right, because he looked incredibly frightened. Another runner tried to pull the driver away from behind, but he turned and punched the boy hard in the nose. I was surprised that it made such a loud noise, and that the driver had managed to keep hold of the other kid's hair while doing it. The boy with the broken nose was trying to push his way through the crowd. I knew he would end up falling before he reached the gate.

Several bottles had been smashed on the ground. To my left a puddle of blood was forming. It ran across the platform towards the tracks. Everywhere there was cursing and angry elated panic and yells for the station cop. And there was laughing too. Someone laughing. I watched my friend Stephan getting trampled by sandaled and booted feet on the cement. All of this happened in what seemed like seconds. Then, finally, I could hear David.

I could almost feel him walking out of the station house, and then I saw him pushing quickly through the crowd, weaving easily around bodies and fists.

Spero was towering above the crowd of runners, yelling in Greek and confident in his ultimate power. A driver. He was unprepared for the blow that was about to be dealt to him. His wide open face half smiling, and a hush falling upon the crowd as David walked up behind him, reached between his legs and grabbed him by the balls. Spero's face came undone and he winced as David wrenched him backwards and threw a punch to the base of his head, knocking him off balance and sending him to the ground.

Just then, the train rolled in with an evil hiss, bringing with it tourists and commuters, their expressions turning to amazement as they looked to the platform. A conductor leaned out of one of the doors, blowing his whistle and calling for the station cops. Several people ventured off the train, running clumsily for the station door. A tall gangly kid got kicked and fell to the ground underneath the weight of his overpacked pack. A few runners fell over him, causing a pile up. The conductor continued to blow his whistle from the door of the train. A few yards away from me another runner got knocked into the bricks face first.

David, who was half a foot shorter than Spero, was now above him, standing on Spero's hand and crushing the side of his face into the platform with the heel of his other foot.

"If you come near us again," he said in a low even tone, "I will kill you."

He pressed hard against Spero's cheek and then stepped back and kicked him several times in the stomach, pausing just slightly between kicks, as if he were practicing their proper placement.

The tangle of limbs had separated and cleared back to watch David take Spero down. None of the other drivers dared to get involved, and none of the runners needed to. Spero pulled himself up on all fours, shook his head and brought himself to a kneeling position. His face was red and puffy. He yelled something in Greek and the other drivers waited for him to stand before strutting awkwardly to the gate, bloody, hurt, some of them grinning, one of them cut badly, his shirt darkly stained.

The train was still waiting. The platform was covered with glass and bloody footprints and leaflets. Greek music was still playing inside the station and could now be heard out on the platform again. The passengers left the train, walking cautiously through the debris, and around the kids who were lying on the concrete. A Greek woman spat at me as she walked by. The boy who had his face bitten was sitting on the bench. I don't know why, he was just sitting there. His cheeks were swollen and covered with blood. I stood up and looked for Danny, ignoring him.

David was surrounded by a crowd of laughing admirers. People were helping their friends get up with dazed expressions. Far down the platform someone sat with his legs crossed on a bench, smoking. I could feel him smiling. He was an American runner from Pireaus, one of the two Americans I had met when I had lived in Athens the year before. I immediately turned my back to him and walked toward the gate.

David spotted me and ran over. "What happened? Did you get cut?"

"No."

"There's blood all over your arm."

I checked first to see if I had a nosebleed. I looked down and there was blood covering my t-shirt and right arm. "It's not mine," I said.

He grabbed my hand and pulled me into the men's room, where he ran water over my arm. It felt good and exposed no cut.

"See?" I said, "It's not my blood." I took off my shirt and threw it in the garbage can near the sink. There was blood on the shoulder and sleeve and spatter marks across the front.

"God, you're skinny, lass. You're a little bone." The words echoed off the tile. I glanced at my reflection in the warped mirror that was bolted to the side of the bricks and then looked away. He gave me his jean jacket to wear and I buttoned it up to the top. The denim was hot and sweaty.

"How can you wear this thing all summer?"

"Just be glad I do. It's saving you the embarrassment of your mates finding out you're really a fourteen-year-old boy."

I laughed.

"This is the worst one in a while," he said. "I'm going to have to talk to that fuck-wit."

"Yeah. You think anyone is really hurt?"

He smirked and shook his head. "I doubt it."

I unbuttoned the first button of the jacket. Put my hands in the pockets looking for cigarettes that wouldn't be there. He ran a hand over my head, lifted my chin with a knuckle and studied me for a minute.

"Suck it up," he said.

"I'm fine."

"You don't look it."
I squared my shoulders and focused just beyond his face.
"Right," he said.
We walked out of the bathroom. Runners were actually getting on to the train to Elephsina. I could see them through the window, packed into the bar car. The conductor leaned out the door. "You on?" he shouted. I ran as the train started moving. David stepped up after me, and we walked down the lurching corridor together.

*

Everyday after the morning run my brother and I would eat creamed chipped beef on toast. Then we would pack our lunches. John would go to the drop zone and I would go to school. I had a teacher then named Mr. Trumble who was very tanned and had dark hair. When we were first introduced mid-year he asked me if I wanted to be a paratrooper like my father.
"My father," I told him, "is dead."
"That's 'my father is dead, sir,'" John corrected. Giving my hand a little squeeze on the word sir. I didn't repeat the sentence.
"I'm very sorry to hear that, son," Mr. Trumble said.
I looked at my brother and he shook his head and started to laugh a little. He didn't have to tell Mr. Trumble what happened to our father, but he could have at least told him I was a girl.
"I'm Achilles," I said to Mr. Trumble. My ankles had been rubbed raw during the morning run and were bleeding into my socks. "Achilles' mom dressed him like a girl so he wouldn't get hurt." I made a muscle.
Mr. Trumble nodded but he looked disturbed. "Well, we're going to be reading about the battle of Troy this year," he said.
"Maybe you are. But I'm not. Sir."
At that my brother lifted me into the air by one arm and carried me to the car. He opened the door and swung me lightly into the passenger side, then closed it and walked back over to talk to Mr. Trumble. I turned the key in the ignition and put the radio on. Then I opened the glove compartment and looked at the car owner's manual, sunk down in the seat and held it in front of my face. So if someone looked

in, they couldn't read my lips.

"Mom," I said. I pulled the front of my shirt up over my mouth and said it one more time. "Mom," I said, like you would begin a story about something you saw.

*

David sat down a few cars behind me and I continued on through the connecting hallways to the bar. I ordered a beer, drank it in a few long gulps and gave the bottle back to the bartender.

"That didn't quite do it," I said to no one, and pulled my crushed cigarettes out of my back pocket. I tried to straighten them for a few seconds, then I just tore the filters off and threw them on the floor. I smoked with loose tobacco on my tongue and stared out the window, feeling the countryside fly by and anticipating the beautiful fire of the foundry to soothe me.

Danny came up and handed me another beer.

"You're okay," I said turning to look at him.

"That was amazing."

"Uhuh. Wait, keep watching. There's something you should see, keep watching outside."

We stood together in front of the window.

"Black towers and yellow fire," he said.

I handed him the new empty.

We were not sober by the time we reached Elephsina. David shook his head in disgust as he watched us tumble out of the train. He went into the tiny rail-side shack, to talk to the official looking Greek men inside. The idiotic singing died hard, and a few people were still trying to keep it going as we sat outside. A German kid from Hotel Larrissia actually started singing "Deutschland Uber Alles," but was stopped short by Stephan who punched him hard in the stomach. The German runner buckled and sat down on the ground.

A Scottish boy named Mike jumped up on a bench and sang "My. name. is Joseph. Gunnar. and. I work. for. Connection. I won't. drink. your. Metaxa. For I. am. a pro-fes-sional. runner."

He rolled the Rs dramatically. Everyone laughed at his mock Dutch accent. Professional runner was the biggest insult you could give someone and Mike made the words sound especially silly. He was a beautiful boy and had an equally beautiful accent. Back in Edinburgh he worked in a greenhouse specializing in bulbs. His arms were strong, and the veins were thick in his neck and hands; in the inside of his biceps, even in the knuckles of his index fingers they were visible. He was lean, and broad chested, with bad teeth, green eyes and long dark hair that was shaved up the back, and pulled into a pony tail. Athens was a place for him to fuck around for the summer. He didn't care how ugly it got, it was all fun for him. He spent one month in Athens and one month on the Islands for the past five summers, and he always ran.

"My name is Maya Brennan," he sang in an American drawl. "I come for a drunken dead man."

Another big laugh. A few people looked at me out of the corners of their eyes, but it was funny, and the accent was perfect.

Mike laughed and stepped off the bench. He took a drink.

"Sorry, My," he said, giggling, "but he'd think it was fuckin funny." He looked down at me and I could see him trying to bring Jezz's image between us, to raise him up.

"No, it's okay," I said. "I mean, it's the truth right?"

I stepped back to look at his smiling face, and then I kicked him hard in the balls with the heel of my boot. He sucked in a mouthful of air and a look of shock came over his face. There was more laughter.

I was surprised that I had kicked Mike. I hadn't considered doing it until it was already happening, until I had raised my knee and felt my throat constrict and a chill on my back. I looked down at him for a while searching for the remains of some emotion. He looked sick. He was kneeling, his shoulders were wide beneath the thin t-shirt he wore and the shaved part of his head was beautiful, the tiny hairs were dirty blond not black. And the back of his neck was very pale. He had boots like mine. Finally, I wandered back over to where I had been standing to wait for the train.

6

A light appeared down the track and we formed lines where the first and last passenger cars would stop. When the train pulled in, we pushed into the compartments sweating and grinning at tourists right and left. Some Greek commuters were sitting with their bundles and briefcases. One couple had a live chicken and many small plastic bags tied with string. They looked angry and sickened as we walked by them.

The train was packed and hot and many people had to stand on their suitcases and packs. They stared at us as we squeezed by.

I got stuck between a compartment door and a line of people and packs that seemed to run the length of the train. It was a horrible car and I pushed around bodies until I was forced to walk on the arms of seats, holding on to the overhead rack. I got through and found another crowd in the next car, not quite as bad. I waited behind a few runners, listening to them, too tired to laugh at their pitch, then followed them into the bar car. Someone had thrown up just inside the doorway, and the first few people through slipped and fell backwards into the vomit. They pulled themselves up on the door frame, wiping their hands and arms on the fronts of their shirts, and continuing on. "Watch for the puke," someone shouted back at us. We stepped around and over and through it and stood in front of the bar fumbling through our pockets for drachmas.

Danny was already standing there with a drink in his hand. I watched him knock back his beer. Things were moving, bright yellow and slick. Glass clinked, and we were reflected in the small rectangular windows on either side of the compartment, and in the silvery metal bar, and all around our faces shone at one another. An exponentially bigger crowd grinning in at ourselves from the darkness of the track. Laughing. Moving faster. Sliding like mercury through the evening, the landscape. But still not fast enough. Hurry up! you want to scream packed in there with all those eyes. Hurry up! Hurry. the. fuck. UP. Jesus Christ! Fuck! C'MON! Holy-mother-of-GOD-hurry-the-fuck-UP! NOW! NOW! Go-go-go-go-go-go-go! You sick. slow. bastards!

*

Our commission had to wait outside, because the lobby could only hold ten people. They lined up on the steps looking sweaty and exhausted under their packs, under the things that they just couldn't part with for a few weeks. Pairs of shoes hung off their shoulders, cameras around their necks, rolled up straw mats to lay down in case sitting on sand or sidewalks was required, bottled water, sunglasses, the secret passport, credit card, and money pouch, visible through the college insignia t-shirts, or the flourescently colored tank tops. They were weighted down, junk hung all over them. And inside the packs it was worse still, ridiculous amounts of socks and underwear, I was sure, travel games, walkmans, silverware, bags to carry dirty clothes in, frisbees, alarm clocks, fifteen shirts, and ten pairs of shorts, not to mention the right clothes for the disco, the hats to keep them from dehydrating too fast, the film, and the plastic film containers now filled with drugs scored in Amsterdam, the travel guides, Eurail passes, the vitamins, conditioners, shampoos, and soaps, perfumes, toothpaste. Condoms, travel mugs, cassettes, mementos of home. The bags to put new souvenirs, new clothing, and other artifacts in. They carried it all, and now they leaned near the door of Olympos, one behind the other, newly exchanged money in hand.

"Do they take our passports?" asked a Danish boy rummaging through the zipper belt at his waist.

Nigel and I laughed hard, every time we looked at each other we started laughing again. The boy stared at us, his eyebrows knit, half smiling.

"No," I said finally, "we used to hold passports, but last year a few of them were stolen."

"Why would they steal passports instead of money?"

Nigel looked at me. "To sell," he told the boy, incredulously. But you could see it still didn't register.

I slipped behind the line of tourists and ran upstairs to my room for a new shirt and a pack of cigarettes, leaving Nigel to deal with Dimitri. I sat in my room for a while feeling dizzy and staring at my boots while my heart pounded. I took out my passport and flipped through the pages for a photograph of my brother I carried. It had his address and phone number on the back. John Brennan. 50 M Hasbrouck Apartments, Ithaca N.Y. 14850. In the photograph he is always twenty-five years old, standing in a field in a baggy green uniform, holding his helmet, the oxygen mask dangling to the side, his light blue chute still connected to him, flattened, out of focus in the background. High altitude, low something...high altitude low...it was HALO training. He squints, his cheeks red, the uniform is marked US SF. The sun hits him and the shadow of his lean body marks the ground with a straight black line.

I would call him later when it was morning there, I thought, before he went to class. Or maybe when it was night. Or maybe something. Maybe I'd forget about it once I sobered up. But there's no chance of that, I thought. Not anymore. I put the picture in my pocket, and stood up throwing the wall on to the ceiling. I strained to focus my eyes and thought what a bad idea it had been to walk upstairs. I would walk it off on the way to Paradise, I thought. I took off David's jacket, pulled another t-shirt out of my bookbag and wrestled it over my head. I stepped out into the hall. My legs had fallen asleep. Uh oh, I thought, trying to close the door. I fumbled with the key for what seemed like hours.

"Maybe if you run you'll feel better," said the key.

"You're right," I said. I turned and pounded heavily and blindly down the stairs.

These boots are keeping me alive, I thought as the tile and twisted railing and column of empty space jerked in and out of sight. I hit the lobby at last.

I ran straight into Nigel. He looked at me and put my commission money into my hand.

"Off to Paradise now?" he said so cool.

"Yeah."

"C'mon I'll walk with you," he said.

The warm night tore through my body as we stepped out. I held Nigel's hand, breathed and felt calmer, but no more coherent.

"Am I too wasted?" I asked him.

"You look like you always do," he said.

*

The bright yellow sign glared Paradise. We walked together through the black and silver room. People were moving slowly and mechanically. First their faces were near, then they disappeared. Over and over again. Nigel went to talk to Mike and Stephan, sliding past moving arms and hands and floating heads. Danny's head sailed into view, stopped and grinned.

"Maya! We killed the train!" he shouted, using a runners' expression he had clearly just learned.

"Uh...hush. Shh."

His face blinked on and off and his smile stayed where it was behind my eyelids. The music boomed out of my chest, got caught against my back and burst out again.

Danny stood beside me smiling and giggling.

Nick Cave's voice resonated from every part of the room. "If this is heaven, I'm bailing out," he screamed. And there was something very familiar about it, as though the song had been written to play right there. An anthem for the neighborhood. For the bar. For the spirit of it all.

"Rats in paradise-ah," he hissed. "Rats in paradise, rats in paradise-ahhh." Each time I heard it it was some kind of blow to the head. The words pulsed with the lights, with Danny's amused and flickering face. I listened without speaking, just waiting. I felt like I might need to go for a run. A long run. I wondered what time it was and what country we were in. The name Jens Christensen popped into my head. A Danish pseudonym for a flesh packaged explosive. Oh, there was something inside of me now too wasn't there?

It's a funny song, said Jezz, *but his later stuff was better.*

"I know." I didn't look at him right away in case he might not be there. But my skin broke out in goose bumps and I was suddenly able to concentrate. I was suddenly calm.

I wonder whose tape this is. I used't have this tape. He wasn't shouting and I could hear him clearly.

"Yeah, I remember," I said.

"My body is a monster driven insane," screamed the singer.

"I love that line," I thought.

Me too, said Jezz. *Me too, baby.*

"Hey," I said, "What ever happened to the money?" The word baby made me think of money and how I needed some.

Had to pay debts. He winked at me but his eyelids were translucent and I could see his eyes through them, just the definition of his light eyelashes gave away the wink, framed it, the slight arc of them falling over his eye and then raising again. He seemed cleaner than before, slighter.

"My heart is a fish toasted in flame," cried Nick Cave viciously.

That bastard woulda killed me. He wanted to. He was workin up to it he was. He really was. I did owe him.

"I know. I know," I said. But I had no idea what he was talking about.

We can still go the islands. We can still travel. You see so much more when you travel like we do. We'll get to Prague, he promised, pulling me closer to him. His smell, his sweat, his brand of cigarettes, it was all real and there. It was overwhelming. *We will. All three of us.*

"We will," I told him waiting for the next line in the song.

"My life is a box full of DIRT." The music slid through my veins like a little flame and exploded painfully into my throat, into my sinus cavities.

Y' know, come to think of it, My, we could actually go really soon. You could make fifteen hundred quid on your papers and have new ones by tomorrow afternoon. We could be gone in twenty-four hours. We could be in Prague by end of the week. He beamed at me.

"It'd be a hell of a lot longer than twenty-four hours. You think the consulate'll just take my word that I lost it? Again? And you know that my brother's address is on the emergency contact page of this one. I just looked at it tonight in fact. It's in ink too. My brother, man. My brother."

So? he shrugged. *Write down the address before you move the thing.* A look of pain came over his face and he broke out in tiny pin pricks of sweat. He held his side, hunched over, his eyes opened wider, unfocused. *Ow. Jesus fuck, this bloody thing still hurts. Holy motherfucking christ, baby.*

I found it weird that he should be able to feel anything. I recognized the expression though, it didn't look like he was kidding. I watched him till the pain subsided and he straightened up.

"Well, anyway," I continued, "I mean.... I don't want to end up like Nigel using someone else's passport to get around. Jesus, get stuck with a stupid name like 'Whipple Perry,' like he did. He's going to have to get that thing renewed in a couple of years, he'll be officially 'Whipple Perry' from Derbyshire for the rest of his life."

Jezz smirked. *Yeah, or he'll get sent to prison the second he tries to renew it. So what?*

"So nothing," I said. "I'm done.

He shrugged. The boy was truly stupid. I hated talking to him about this stuff. I wished he hadn't brought it up and he knew it. Christ, who was he to talk about getting somewhere?

Ah, well, he said. *Hardly matters now, does it?* He shrugged. He was eager to see how I treated him under his newly deceased status. He shoved his hands in his pockets, opened his eyes and rocked on his heels. He leaned his forehead against mine, trying to create some kind of macabre effect. I couldn't smell liquor, though his lips were practically touching mine.

You missed me by a couple of days, he whispered. I could hear him just fine. He was making such an effort at being a spirit, with great subtlety and sincerity; I thought maybe he was sober now in death. Maybe he'd be good at this, like he'd been at piano. He was certainly making me feel like shit. I was sure that was one of the more important things about being dead, making other people feel like shit.

"No, no, baby, you missed me," I said. "One less pint and we'd be out of here, passports got nothing to do with it."

Maybe forty less, he grinned back. *They call it Ouzo 10 because you should be within ten minutes of a hospital if you intend to finish it.* He winked again.

"Where'd they bury you?"

In the back garden by the garage.

"What?"

He laughed. *You've got the obituary. Dunnit say?*

"I don't think so. Doesn't say much. You died suddenly."

He laughed. *Yeah, that's accurate.*

I could see him more clearly. He was wearing jeans and a white t-shirt and his hair was short and blond and clean. He was the only one in the room that refused to be swallowed and spat back out by the lights. He was still beautiful. Tall and skinny, skinnier than I ever remembered, but he probably lost a lot of weight being unconscious.

He was pale, shaven, he had obviously taken a bath since the last time I had seen him. His full curled lips stretched around a gap-toothed, nicotine stained grin. I knew there was something I had to tell him but I couldn't remember it. I lifted my face for a kiss.

Wanna see a trick? he asked, pulling a coin out of his pocket.

"No." I closed my eyes.

Aw...You don't miss me do you? he thought.

"I don't know. Jesus. Of course I do. What the fuck?"

Did you come back because you missed me?

"Jesus," I said. I couldn't remember what it was I had to tell him about us.

I had just wanted a kiss and still did.

Can I have a fag? he asked, *I've been smoking these Navys for so long. Let's have a real taste of tobacco.*

I reached into my pocket for my pack, put two cigarettes in my mouth and lit them. Just then I remembered what it was I had to tell him, under our circumstances, separated by his non-existence and all, he'd find it pretty hilarious. I took one of the cigarettes out of my mouth and looked up to hand it to him, but he was gone. I smoked them both and fell asleep standing up. Smoking for two now.

*

"Collect call from Maya, will you accept?"

"Yes, ma'am."

"Hello?"

"Hey Little Bone! Where are you?!"

"Back in Greece."

"Have you got an address yet?"

"Not really."

"Well, how are you?!"

"Great. It's hot here. I got a job at a hotel."

"That's great! You are one squared away motherfucker, Brennan."

I nodded. "It's beautiful. Athens is pretty dirty, but still...I had a nice trip over the Med on my way here. The stars were...."

"You've got to write me."

"I know I'm sorry about the call. I just wanted to see if everything's still there."

"Yep, everything still is. School's out in another week. I'm getting finals nailed shut and then its back to Benning for two weeks. It's not Greece though."

"Yeah."

"When are you coming home?"

"I don't know, when I've seen enough, I guess. You'd love the Acropolis and the Parthenon."

"Yes I would, dog body."

"I better let you go."

"Alright, Bone."

"Love you."

"I love you, Maya, you be good."

"I will."

I left the OTE with its thousands of telephones and made my way back to Victor Hugo Street. Then I ran.

7

I got back to Olympos and was greeted by Sterious, sitting in his sweater, scowling.

"I made coffee. You want?"

"Yes, please."

He handed me a little cup and with an angry expression he spooned sugar into it, stirring it roughly while I held it. I was tired.

"Can I have my key?" I asked, drinking the shot and wiping my mouth on my arm.

He turned and looked at the board of hooks behind him. "Maya has your key," he said distractedly.

I fished through my pockets. "No, I don't. I must have left the door open." I started up the stairs. "Good night," I said.

He scoffed, as he spooned more dark powder into the little green cup in front of him.

*

My room was unlocked. I went in and sat on my cot. There was a body in the bed near the balcony, white with sunburned forearms. I untied my boots, unwound the laces from around my ankles and went over to see who it was.

"Hey!" I yelled into its ear.

Danny rolled over and groaned. The balled-up jeans he had been using for a pillow, and his face, were wet with saliva. His cheeks were creased from the seams in the jeans. He looked too sweaty. Too well rested.

"What are you doing in my room?"

"I got kicked out of Anabells."

"How?"

"Seems I behaved poorly."

"Oh?"

He wiped his face and arched his back.

"How did you get in?" I asked.

"I came looking for you. That fat guy gave me the key. He said he's some kind of flag expert or something. Made me quiz him on the flags of the world and then wait while he spat out the answers. He's got a stutter. Then he offered me a job running and gave me the key. When I got up here there was another key hanging in the door, yours I guess. Where did you wander off to last night?"

"We don't need another runner."

"Hm."

"There's only two rooms up here for runners. You can stay with Nigel."

"Do you want some espresso?" he asked.

"Sure," I said. I thought he was joking.

He undid his pack and pulled out a little propane camping stove and set it up. Then he pulled out a tin of coffee and a two cup espresso maker. He handed me the bottom of the pot and I filled it at the sink, watched him pack it and light the stove.

I was impressed so I made sure not to comment on it. I searched through my bag for another box of smokes. "Man, you have so much stuff."

"Yeah, it's a big pain in the ass, but I camped all the way down here, so I really needed most of it."

I lit a cigarette on the blue flames of the propane burner and watched him as he sat in bed drinking his coffee. He had a muscular body, broad shouldered and defined. He had no hair on his chest or face, a wide jaw, full lips and deep set dark eyes. If Caravaggio had painted boy scouts they would have looked like Danny.

"How old are you?"

"Twenty-six," he said.

"Really? I thought you were much younger."

"How old are you?"

"Guess."

"Twenty-three? Twenty-four? Twelve?"

"Eighteen."

"I can never tell how old girls are."

"That's bad for you," I said, knocking back the espresso. I lay on my bed, and looked at the patterns in the ceiling. It was a Greek key. It had no beginning and no end.

I woke up alone in the dark. I felt shaky and my head was pounding. I was nauseated, dehydrated. I had missed the train. I lay in bed watching the shadows in the room, smoking. I didn't know if it was twilight or dawn. I felt a chill.

This was familiar. Some nightfall from a long time ago. Some dark room in some housing complex on some base of operations. I remembered the heat turning on and the TV flickering, shifting the patterns on the rug. I read, with the sound off. I've been reading *The Castle*. I'm hungry but I can't make myself go turn on the light, so I get a package of stale crackers from where I left them under the couch. No one has come home to make dinner. For now I just wait. I say the word "Mom" because I haven't heard it in a long time and want to. I say "Mom," just like you would, to begin telling her a story, but I don't know what to say after that so I just shut up.

I didn't like TV at all, even when I was little, even when I first moved to base. But I did like *Battle of the Planets*. Four orphans in bird costumes fight an army lead by a hermaphrodite named Zoltar. The main character of the cartoon, as I saw it, was a girl named Princess. There were three boys in her squad and they were named G-force.

In the opening credits it called them "four brave young orphans" but later you found out they weren't orphans at all. Every once in a while someone's mother or father would turn up.

It was not as good as *The Castle*. It was not even as good as *The Trial*. But it was good to have on sometimes for company. Often I got the plots confused with things I was reading. When I pictured the characters from my *Timeless Tales of Gods and Heroes* book they looked like the G-force team. Achilles looked like Princess. And I imagined her mother lovingly holding her over the fire to make her immortal. I imagined it, while I watched the show. Little Princess Achilles doesn't get to be immortal, though, because her father kills himself, to make her mother miserable. It doesn't work of course, it just makes her mother leave. You never saw her father to begin with. He was just some clothes hanging, shoe trees without the shoes, a handful of change on the counter. But her mother was the main character of the myth, so you noticed when she was gone.

Achilles was better than Princess. But Princess looked like me. And she had a team like my brother had. She wore a white and pink minidress and white gloves, and a helmet with a visor shaped like a beak. When she killed the soldiers she extended her arm, shot them in the head and cartwheeled away. She had dark hair like mine. She fought hard.

On base waiting for my brother, I would fall asleep on the floor in front of the quiet vespers of the television. And I would dream that I was Princess, or Achilles, or Joseph K. And that I was with my team.

*

Danny came back, opening the door, bringing warm wind, and a bright, melancholic artificial glow to the yellowing walls.

"Hey, I tried to wake you for the train." He had been drinking and his voice was slow and easy.

"What time is it?"

"Ten-thirty. I just got in."

" Did you get anyone?"

"I got two Swedes." He turned on the light and closed the door. "Nigel didn't do the train either, and I don't know what the hell I'm doing."

"Don't worry," I told him.

"Want some coffee?" he asked.

"Yeah," I said, sitting up and lighting a cigarette. Overcome by the need to vomit I ran to the balcony. I stood there and breathed for a while. I got it under control this time.

When I came back he was sitting cross legged on his bed making the coffee, carefully pushing the propane stove away from his sleeping bag.

"You okay?" he asked, glancing up.

"Mmhm."

He pulled books and maps out of his pack, putting them in separate stacks in front of him. I looked at him. He was like no one I had ever wanted to know. He was like one of those athlete boys who go to college. There was something soft about his fitness and it spoke of mirrors. His body was like a toy version of what a man's body should look like, an approximation of something made by work. His was a body built with country club memberships and then used as a mannequin to display certain types of clothes. He was one of leisure's grotesque little whores. Their self-conscious confidence, their knowing look and swagger hinting at sexual competence, that they could only achieve if they were a photograph and you had a free hand. Dannyboy was not made for real work of any kind. And the way he had worked on himself was simply base.

"Like what you see?" he asked sarcastically. Looking at me with a smirk.

I laughed.

He shook his head. "David was worried that you weren't on the train. He might stop by later." He threw some books on my bed. "Do you want these? I've got to start unloading some of this shit."

"I can't believe I missed the train," I said. "I'm out a thousand drachmas. Just earlier I was saying how I need to start saving."

I looked at his books. Delicate and worn, or shiny and important. Finally he threw *The Possessed* on to my bed with its plain brown and black paperback cover. I smelled the pages.

"Thank you," I said. "I love Dostoevsky." And for a moment he didn't look so ugly .

"That kid, Tom," he said.

"Who?"
"The one who got boxed."
"Yeah?"
"He was on the train. He got a bunch of stitches, but somehow his jaw wasn't broken."
"Lucky."
He pulled more stuff out of his pack. He had Shampoo.
"How did you lug that thing around for so long?" I asked.
"I think 'why' is more the question."
"What did you do back home?"
"Nothing. Graduated college. Moved in with my parents till I had enough money to leave."
"What did you study?"
"History."
"Why?"
"I don't know. You have to pick something."
"Do you want to go see some Greek dancing?"
"I'd love to."
He shoved his pack back under the bed and I grabbed my last box of cigarettes. I packed them against the side of my right hand, took a drink from the tap, wet my face and hair, grabbed David's jean jacket off the floor, and we left to pick up the man. Our man in Athens. Our David Joyce, whose grandfather was James Joyce! You know how many James Joyces there are in Ireland? There's more than one.

*

"Why weren't you on the train?" David asked me.
"Overslept."
"You mean unconscious," he said. It was a statement that I had misspoken, and needed to correct it. His face was set in a deliberate mask of thinly veiled rage. A joke, but only if you went along with it. Only one reply.
"That's right," I said looking straight into his eyes. "I was unconscious."
"Thank you for returning my jacket." He put it on, raised his eyebrows and his face broke into a disarming smile. Danny and I fol-

lowed him through the double antique doors of Athens Inn and out into the night.

"We'll head down your way then to Popodopolous?" David asked. "That's what you want?"

"That's what I want," I said.

The restaurant had a raised terrace, just off Diligianni. A grape trellis ran overhead and unripe grapes hung down over the tables. Danny picked one and ate it, wincing from the sour taste. Then he ate two more, spitting part of the last one into his napkin.

We sat at a white plastic table and looked at the red paper place mats that also served as menus.

I couldn't read the menu which was very faint and blurry, and I realized I was looking at the wrong side, trying to read it backwards through the paper. I flipped it over, looking up at David just as he averted his eyes. There were a few tables of tourists drinking retsina and eating grape leaves. There were a few Greek couples finishing a meal despite the hour. Instrument cases were piled in a corner near the kitchen entrance, and loud conversation could be heard from inside. I lit a cigarette and handed it to Danny who seemed to be eager to pick up the habit.

The waiter came and shook hands with David, who ordered water and beer for us, and a pastitio for me.

"Listen Americans," David said. "What's the connection between acne and Catholic Priests?"

"I dunno," said Danny. "What?"

"Neither of them come on your face till you're eleven." He raised his eyebrows, closed one eye and clenched his teeth.

Danny laughed, and I laughed even though I'd heard him tell it before.

"Where's the dancing?" Danny asked.

"When the band gets back."

"Maya could dance," said Danny. "She's already got the kicks down."

"How's that?" I asked.

"Mike."

"What about him?"

"Oh yes, yes," David said. "It's a reflex, you know. It's a good reflex to have."

"What are you talking about?"

"You ground your heel into Mike's balls," Danny said.

"I don't think so," I said.

"Oh, it's lovely," David said. "I'm sorry I wasn't right there."

"So am I. When did I kick Mike?"

"Last night, I think."

"You can always tell the children of servicemen," David said lovingly. "Look at her."

"Was your father in the army?" Danny asked.

"No."

"Look at her," David said. "I could tell the second I met her." He was getting nostalgic.

"Yeah?" Danny asked. "How?"

"Because of our great restraint," I said taking my Amstel off the waiter's tray as he came by. I drank the pint in several gulps, not taking my lips away from the bottle.

"Was one of your parents in the army?"

"No," I said again, putting the empty down.

"Her brother," David told him. "Those are the best behaved kids you'll ever see—Army kids. I'm serious. The whole society should be raised like this. A whole world of Brennans."

Danny smiled. A look of ironic interest passed over his face as he registered this information.

"Ah, looka this," David said. "Look at him. He'll fall in love despite the warning I just gave him." He slapped him on the back. "I said this before and I'll say it again. Stay away from her." He smiled. "Or you'll wake up without a head." He laughed and Danny laughed too and tilted his bottle back. "I'm not kidding," David added, still grinning, and sounding like he was.

I watched the cars speed by on the street below the terrace. Then looked down at my lap.

Our food came and I drank another Amstel. The musicians came out of the kitchen and picked up their mandolins and bazoukis, and started to play. The music was too fast and too complicated. But when it was part of the dance, It all seemed complete. It filled me with a real sense of joy to watch bodies moving perfectly to the drum and strings, touching each other and jumping and laughing. It always made me want to learn the dances. It always made me wish I was Greek.

They played for quite a while before the couples who had been sitting got up and began to push tables and chairs out of the way, clearing a small circle to the side of the band. They carried their plates and bottles inside and came back clapping and smiling. Dark eyed women with graying hair and strong shoulders, and men with shiny wet looking hair and button down shirts, and their grown children. This was their neighborhood. It was their bad neighborhood.

They formed a half circle, linking their arms around each other's shoulders, and started with a simple metered cross step. The men at the end of the line held white handkerchiefs in their outstretched hands, and waved them. The sounds of their heels hitting the terrace became part of the music, and their dance grew faster, their bodies still bouncing in perfect unison. I loved to watch the men dance. The fat men, and the old men, and the men with too much jewelry and mustaches, and the young, handsome men. I loved to watch them doing the same dances as the wives, moving with equal power and control, arms linked or hands held, feet stomping at the same moment, smiling, sweating and a little drunk in their city at night.

The songs spun to a stop and they stood breathing. Waiting for the next one. The traffic was audible again. I went to the kitchen and brought back more beer for me and Danny. My belly was full and I felt keenly aware. They began the next song, and we sat back, admiring them. They formed a circle within a circle. Spiraling in opposite directions. Drawing close together and then spreading out, almost hitting the tables, their arms still linked. I felt like laughing. I could feel the people living in the buildings and out at the cafes and driving in their cars. Living everywhere, this beautiful race of creatures that plays and speaks, and invents dances. This beautiful race that knows thousand-year-old dances.

"This is excellent," Danny shouted, leaning in towards the table.

"That it is," David agreed. "That it is."

*

The people that bought stolen documents weren't so different from the man at the consulate who reissued mine, they were smarter but just as caught up in the aesthetic posturing of their trade. Jezz never managed to interact with them without getting hurt. It was like a handshake. Every fucking time. He made people paranoid. He would exaggerate how many he had or not remember which nationality, and invariably they would think he was screwing them.

We didn't quite get what happened to the passports after we got our money. Or why it mattered. Why passports even existed. It was part of someone else's fucked up world, an ugly ill-conceived world that co-existed with ours, but in no way touched it. It was hard to believe that these little books were so important, these 'official' identity documents. They were yellow stars or visa cards, depending on who you were and where you were from. They meant nothing.

But they could provide enough money to see Istanbul, or to buy bicycles, or to go to the islands and come back. It was a way to never go home. The perfect way to stay in motion. A way to really study, live in our books and our drinks, and our visions. And we didn't go looking for this money, it was providence that Jezz ever got his hands on any passports in the first place. It had been a joke. It had all been a joke, right from the beginning.

Dimitri had been logging the numbers of several passports in the hotel registry. We'd brought in a large group of Danes and they were sleeping on the roof. He made them all leave their passports for some reason. He was afraid they wouldn't pay for the roof unless we had something of theirs they needed back. He shook his head vigorously as he made his list of numbers. He wouldn't give us any commission until he had them all down. And the entire time he talked about Sterious.

"H-h-he is a-a....a senile. N-n-never he does th-th-this work. Only me. Only I do it. He he he is senile."

"As well as being pure evil," Jezz said, smiling at him, leaning on the desk. "Senile and evil. Don't forget about evil."

"Y-y-you don't know h-how bad h-h-he is."

"Be reasonable now, Dimitri. If Sterious is, as we've all heard, a dead man brought back to life, you may judging him by the criteria of the living, and so he only seems bad. But for a dead man he may be exceptional in his demeanor."

At this point Dimitri gave us a hateful look and began to ignore us, putting down numbers and then stacking the documents to the side.

Jezz said, "is it true? Is he a monster?"

Still Dimitri said nothing. When he looked down to write the next number in the register Jezz slid one of the passports off the top of the pile. He did this quietly a few times when Dimitri was looking down, then he'd glance up at me with raised eyebrows. It was so funny. And the whole while he was doing this he was talking so Dimitri would try harder to ignore him—so that he would glower into the register.

"Speaking of monsters," Jezz went on, "do you have any idea how big my cock is? Talk about a monster. Jesus Christ. Tell him, My."

"It's true, Dimitri."

"If you give us our commission I'll let you see it. You'll only have to pay what you already owe us."

Dimitri said nothing. Jezz shrugged at me.

"I heard that Sterious was actually dug out of a shallow grave near the OTE," he said sliding another document off the pile. "And that the top floor of Olympos was destroyed by the same lightening that reanimated him!" He took a passport and tossed it quietly from hand to hand in front of Dimitri's downcast eyes, then put it in his pocket. "And after that, his demented creator dressed him in the most terrifying costume—a wool cardigan sweater. But as he's the living dead he never feels how fucking hot it is in Greece!" Jezz was screaming at this point. And shouting Ha! to punctuate his statements. "Then his creator gave him orthopedic shoes! And black horn. Rimmed. Glasses. With a little black rope so he wouldn't lose them, Ha! A hideous Frankenstein! A m-monst-ster!"

"G-g-get out!"

"You want us to leave?"

"Go n-n-n-now."

Jezz shrugged. "Okay." He looked at me, shaking his head in happy disbelief. He gave me the passports and I put them in my back pocket. We walked out and down the steps, headed for the bar.

"What do you think Sterious could have done to him?" I asked.

"Who cares?"

We laughed our way to Drinks Time to meet Jack. From the street we could see him, sitting in the window reading. His feet propped up on the table. Three beers already set up.

We opened a few of the documents and looked at them right there in the bar. Jens Christensen. He was Danish, but had black hair and olive skin. He had brown eyes. He was born in Arhus in 1967, and had only two stamps on his passport, one from Germany and the other Greece. Jack looked at it for a while.

"Looks like his mum's Egyptian," he said. "Look at him."

We did.

"I'll bet you could get two thousand quid for it," he said.

*

David's knife was heavy, with a black polished metal handle. The blade was shiny silver, serrated on one side with curved arcs that came to a point, like waves. By four in the morning we had reached the door of Olympos and sat on the steps outside the reception office. David on the top step and I between his legs on the lower one, with my back to him, resting my arms on his knees. He was holding the comb, and the knife lay on the steps at our side.

Danny sat next to us, smoking and gazing at the luminous face of the station clock across the street. He was dazed. He was paralyzed with drink.

"So what did he say?"

"Hold still, lass," he said as he combed through my short knotted hair. "Put your head down."

"Just tell me."

"Ah, Jesus. You're fuckin morbid." He combed more roughly, pausing to pull clumps of hair out of the comb and blow them on to the sidewalk. "It's fuckin boring. Why'd you wanna hear what he said to me? I'm sure he had loving last words for Jack. So there he is, drunk in the morning as usual. He has the shakes, can't shut up. He's standin around with alla them same as everyday, 'watch me trick,' 'look at me' and all. For a minute I thought he was taking the piss or choked on the magic coin from his trick, but he had passed out cold. Right there on the platform in the middle of all his talkin. So I carried him back to his room."

"And?"

"And," he said sarcastically. "I rolled him up in a nice clean sheet, and laid him out upon the bed, with a gallon of ouzo at his feet and a barrel of Amstel at his head," he chuckled. "Now hold still."

"Did you talk to him?"

He laughed suddenly. A genuine belly laugh. I could feel his body shake. And he stopped combing.

"Did you talk to him or not?" I laughed.

"Yep," he laughed even harder."

"What did he say?"

David made a gurgling choking sound. "That's what he said."

It was funny. "No, c'mon what did he say?"

"Tell Maya...I...love...her."

I laughed. "No, really what?"

He was still laughing when he took a deep breath and rubbed his eyes with a flat hand. Then he held the knife in his teeth and pushed me forward, squaring my shoulders, holding my head still. He sighed, a few more laughs. He patted my back gently.

"Please," he said quietly.

"Please what?"

"Please. That's it. He said please. Go figure."

I said nothing. Then it was quiet, back to the business at hand. It was a good anecdote up until the "please" part. I'd cut that part out if I ever talked about it.

David pulled the few inches of my hair up tight. I could feel my scalp raising. Then he slid the blade across and it made a sound I could both hear and feel from inside my skull. An inch or so of hair fell to the step. He repeated this till I had a proper cut. Pulling my scalp, and letting it go.

"If your hair gets too long it'll affect your hearing," he said. "You're not stupid and you're not scared." He said some more things but I wasn't listening. It was relaxing. I liked the part about not being scared. I liked the headlights of the cars driving by. I liked the sound of the knife against my hair. Somehow it reminded me of helping my brother build a pen for our new dog. The dog we never had.

Our yard was long and narrow, and the dog we never had was to live in the back, behind a sycamore tree. John stood on the top step of a small ladder he had secured in the mud, and I stood below him, holding the long metal stakes with a pair of work gloves. *Keep your head down,* he said, and he swung the sledge hammer over his shoulder and down on to the stake. It made my hands sting. There were six stakes to pound. *If I miss you'll never know,* he said. *But I won't ever miss, Bone.*

"Who are you?" David asked quietly.

"Hmm?'

"Who are you now that you're alone?" Hair fell around me and on to my shoulders. I thought for a moment that he was talking to himself, but he really did want an answer. "Who?" he asked again. "Why did you go to Israel? Why is your name Brennan? So I'll like you?"

He was done cutting and now he ran the blade over my head for stray hairs, and up the back of my neck, to get a closer shave at the base of my head. I felt him touch the tip of the blade just behind my ear for a moment. I felt his paranoia radiate out of his pores. But it would stop soon.

Danny was now fully focused on us. Every time I glanced over he was looking meaningfully into my eyes with his own dark wet eyes. Like he was trying to crawl into my skin.

"Who are you?" David asked again.

"Maya Kathleen Brennan."

"Why did you pick that name?"

"That is my name."

"What's your mother's maiden name?"

"O'Shea."

"Who am I?" he asked, like I'd forgotten already.

"I don't know you," I said.

"What's my name?"

I closed my eyes. "You never told me."

"What do I look like?"

"I never saw you."

"Where do I live?"

"I don't know."

He wiped the stray hairs off his knife by rubbing it against his jeans, and then snapped it back into its leather case and hooked it back to his belt. He rubbed his hands roughly over my head to shake out the tiny hairs. Then placed his hands on my shoulders and held me still in front of him. Just held me there.

"I was your age when I joined up," he said. "I cut me hair like this. It improved me hearing. It improved me mind. You have to be completely alert to make sacrifices," he said. "Hear me?"

I nodded, but it was too late to be sitting around on the steps talking about hair. I was beginning to dream about Princess as I sat there. She lived underground. She would hunt the ghosts of deer and live on their meat. She would swim with her team, through the earth, to drink blood from little pools. I watched her drink with her wings unfolding. Men stood beside the pools and asked if she'd seen their sons. She had, she told them. Their sons were always there, beneath the surface, silent, unrepentant and full of forgetting. They had no more base, no more planes, no more passports no more syntec. Their sons lived on asphodels now and couldn't hunt anymore, couldn't swim, had no taste for blood. The men wept to think their sons had no taste for blood. Because that was what they lived on when they were alive.

"Wake up, lassie. Yer startin' to slouch."

I stood and shook the hair off of my clothes, and kicked the pile of brown fuzz into the street. I ran my hands over my head. What was left of my hair was incredibly soft.

David gave me a kiss on the forehead. "Right then, off you go, sleepy lass."

"See you tomorrow," I told him. I hugged him tight. I left Danny sitting on the steps, but he followed me in. They do that. They have transparent faces and they follow you. But not my squad. Not my team of ghosts.

I looked at the stairs, at the dim little lamp burning in the lobby. I'm sure Jezz did have loving last words for Jack. But it's irrelevant. Our squad is gone. Fuck it. Fuck our squad, my friends... My friends are gone. If I were Jack.... If I had no money and no passport, and my boyfriend was dead, where would I be?

Jesus fuck. I'd be hiding. I'd be looking for me. I'd be alone, falling to earth, with no one's hands locked around my wrists, no wrists to lock my hands around.

*

Right, female. This is where you'll be staying. He opened the door to the balcony, and kicked some of the bottles over to the side then threw my poncho liner over the rail. *You must behave yourself. This is my brother, Jack. You may have heard of Jack Rollock. He's a famous midweight queer and has won several queer awards for hitting other men in the face at a small gymnasium in Manchester.* Jezz was very drunk. We'd stopped at Drinks Time before going to the hotel.

Jack unscrewed the cap on a bottle of ouzo and handed it to me and I drank a few sips. Jezz took it from me and held it, still talking and occasionally pausing to drink.

You don't look anything alike, I said.

He's a poet as well. As well as being a model, as well. Can't you see?

Jack held out his hand. Jack Rollock, he said as if Jezz wasn't in the room. *Maya,* I said shaking his hand. He pulled a bottle of Amstel out from under his bed and uncapped it, handed it to me. He sat cross-legged on the little bed with a copy of the *Athens Times* spread out in front of him, a pencil tucked behind his ear. Books and notebooks were piled beside the pillow and beside the metal legs of the bed frame.

Thank you.

Where've you come from, like? he asked.

The States, I said. *By way of Italy, and some other places.*

You're so little. You look tired, like. He paused to light a cigarette. *Evenin's lovely here once the temperature drops. He won't be sober till mornin, but we go out and wander like, stroll, yeah? How do they say it in Italy the passa giatta, like? We go walk up around Monasturaki Square. It's good to get out. The lights shine on the Acropolis, like, its real fine.*

Sounds great.

Are you travelin alone then?

Yeah.

Yeah, we were too.

What're you reading? I asked him.

This? Just looking in the ads for a better place for meself and this charmer. And this is some poetry, do you fancy it? I thought these circumstances, like, were good for learning it, yeah? We've a lot of free time and free rent and the city's just too hot to walk around in all day. In a way you see how poverty is this blessing, like. Good for your character, yeah? If we were all living like this, with nothing. How smart we'd be, yeah, and loving like. Ultimately nothing's what you want.

The last ffucking thing in the ffucking world I want is nothing, Jezz said. His eyes were crossed, bloodshot and watery. He sat down in the middle of Jack's paper and leaned back fishing through his pockets for something. He seemed to forget what he was looking for. He started laughing to himself. Eventually he lay down and closed his eyes.

Jack brushed Jezz's sweaty hair back from his forehead, and reached behind the bed for another Amstel.

You're like a little fairy, Jack said to me. I thought at first he was talking to Jezz. *With your pointy face, and your big eyes.* He started laughing, and then lectured on about nothing.

8

Dimitri was running the desk when we got back from my hair cut. "You are r-running the m-m-morning tr-train from C-Corinthos," he told us. "Y-you leave i-in two hou-hours. Here is train f-fare."

"Fuck," Danny said.

"That's fine," I said. "I need to make some money. Someone stole my commission money the other night."

"You will n-not b-b-be paid un-unless you run the morning tr-train and the thr-three o nnnine." He shouted at us, shaking his head from side to side with his back hunched over and his head down. He didn't even look at us he just shouted.

"That's fine," I told him again.

"And D-Danny, m-must a-also go r-run from C-c-Corinthos. S-so you know h-how t-t-to do it." He glanced up at Danny still shaking his head from side to side.

"How hard can it be?" asked Danny. "I buy a ticket for Corinth and get off when I get there."

We walked back out the door and down to Drinks Time. The sky was a light purple color and we had almost reached the door of the bar when we realized it would be closed. Our train left at six a.m. so we had time to get coffee and bread, though we would probably end up waiting at the station cafe in Corinth anyway.

"It's a bad run from Corinth," I told Danny. "They hate you by the time you're in Athens."

We sat and smoked. I was going to vomit from exhaustion, and the usual thing. I put out my cigarette and tried to keep it down.

"What did you do back home?" he asked me.

"For the last six months I was there I had a paper route."

"Did you go to school?"

"No, my brother did after the army. We lived in student housing at Cornell. I graduated high school early and we were supposed to start college together. But instead I got a paper route. I don't like school. I liked running the route every morning, though. Up around these rich people's houses on this hill."

"Do you get homesick?" he asked.

"No."

For a moment I thought that I was dreaming. The light, the coolness of the street. Danny's perfect English, perfect articulation. My stomach had settled all at once and I didn't need to concentrate on it anymore.

"How long were you in Italy?" he asked. I wasn't interested in the conversation. I looked at him and wondered vaguely if I could do more push ups than he could.

"Five months," I said.

"What did you do there?"

"I worked in a restaurant. I ate gelato like I drink beer here. Probably even more, and not just cones either, sundaes; mostly tiramisu. That is the only thing I did besides work. I actually had to stop drinking there because it cut into the money for gelato."

"Why did you leave?"

"I don't know."

We could smell bread baking as the street got lighter. We stood outside a shop window looking in at the men setting enormous trays of bread and pastries on a counter to cool. Finally, one of them opened the door. We bought chocolate milk and bread and coffee and headed for Larissis to get our train. I bought a pack of Navys on the way, a bearded sailor in blue on the box was ringed with the words 'nay sir, be not angry.'

It would take an hour to get to Corinth. The morning countryside was dry and yellow and full of gnarled shrubs and trees with narrow twisted trunks. Hills rose and fell as the train flew by. We sat silently, watching out the window. Smoking and eating.

*

Our first apartment was nice but not like a house. I slept on the couch. And when I would wake up late at night or early in the morning there would be snow on the TV, bright black and white, and a sibilant sound and my brother would carry me to bed. Sometimes I would wake up and put water on for tea and he would hear me and come down. We would drink tea, eat bread and play crazy eights before it was morning. I wore my pajamas every day for two weeks, and my clear plastic gummy shoes with daisies on them, and my bathing suit underneath all of it. I didn't like to change my clothes. But when school started he insisted. I had to wear clean clothes every day. And he threw away my pajamas. I still wasn't allowed to smoke. I outgrew my gummy shoes and he wouldn't buy me a new pair.

He bought me boxes and boxes of models from the billets. If I couldn't get to sleep he would let me stay home the next day and build models. Glow in the dark monster models. Wolfman, the mummy... and he'd write me an excuse for school.

He would take me out to the drop zone and I would watch him fall to the earth, alone or holding wrists with Sergeant Reese and Private Griswald.

He would walk past the bench after he landed, take off his gloves and slap me on the back of the neck as he walked by. But one time he just stopped and looked at me. He took of his gloves and put a hand on my forehead.

He said *My God, Maya, you're burning.* The light reflecting off a plane played on the side of his face and in the shiny part of his eyes. The wind was picking up a little and I watched the short blades of grass move. He touched my hands. *Even your hands are burning.* He ran into the DZ and got me some Tang with an ice cube in it. He got me his jacket and put it around my shoulders. The jacket felt cool.

It's okay, he said. *I got four more jumps and then we'll go home. Nothing can happen to you, right? You're the toughest kid in the world. Four feet of steel, I'll tell you what. You hear me?*

Four feet of fever, I said.

He buttoned his jacket up around me. *Suck it up,* he said and gave a sharp tug on my hair.

I looked away from the window into the compartment. Nobody was going to Corinth at this hour. Why the hell was I?

9

Danny startled awake, his eyes snapping open.

"C'mon," I said, pulling him up.

We walked through the train and then down to the platform. Danny stretched, yawned and smelled his arm pits.

"Do I smell?" he asked.

"A little. No worse than anyone else."

We walked through the station house and out on to a patio just next door, where we sat and waited for the little cafe to open so we could drink some iced coffee. I wished for a deck of cards, or a set of dominos. Minutes later the cafe opened and Danny went inside, returning with two pints.

"H-h-here is y-your A-a-a-Amstel," he said.

"Oh. That was really good. I don't want beer yet though."

"Y-y-you w-will n-need it for the tr-train."

"You sound just like him."

He raised his bottle. "Cheers," he said raising his bottle.

I spilled a drop on the ground and then drank.

"How much do you weigh?" he asked

"Forty-seven kilos."

"So how many can you drink?"

"Eight, maybe ten, it depends."

"People here seem to drink all day," he said.

I nodded, "and all night."

We sat with our bottles, squinting in the morning light, and feeling the day get hotter.

"Jesus Christ," I said, almost spitting my beer.

"What?"

"Oh, fuck, they must have been in a different car on the way here," I said pointing towards the door of the station.

A tall kid with bad posture and a short brown beard stood with his friend, who looked like a beige blur from where we were sitting. It was Allen.

"I saw that guy during the fight with the drivers," said Danny. "It was weird as hell, he was just sitting there, like it was a movie or something. Nobody touched him. He just sat there. He didn't do a fucking thing."

"They're horrible," I said.

"Who are they?"

"Allen and Lewis. I thought I saw him before too, but I can't believe they're still here. They must run only the morning trains."

"Where are they from?"

"Some hostel out in Pireus."

"No, I mean, what country?"

"The States. New Jersey," I whispered. "Fuck, they saw us."

Allen and Lewis walked towards our table waving and grinning in feigned cordiality and surprise.

"Hi!" they yelled in unison.

"Hey you two," I said drinking my beer quickly and looking at the door of the station.

"Maya, did you hear about Jezz?" Allen asked with studied concern, almost unable to conceal his smile.

His voice was high pitched and nasal, but also gravely sounding. He spoke with the inflection of some nineteen twenties diva who was always bored. He had a permanent crease in his forehead from the strain of keeping a look of false cheer on his face. I had watched him get vicarious pleasure out of people's pain before. Now he was going to do it with me. That was why Allen loved Athens. There were enough people falling down and he could go back to Pireaus and jerk off thinking about it.

"Yes, how are you?" Lewis asked, rubbing my back. He was slightly overweight.

"I'm great," I said.

"Your hair looks beautiful," Lewis said in a tone indiscernible from sarcasm. "It really brings out your eyes, and your jaw line."

"Yeah," I said. "This is the best haircut I've ever had."

They sat at our table.

"Who is your friend?" Lewis asked.

"Ah, this...is Giovanni," I said.

"Hello," Danny said, in an Italian accent.

"He doesn't speak English," I said.

"Where is he from?" Lewis asked.

"Perugia."

Danny nodded and smiled obliviously.

"Tell him I love the candy in Perugia."

"Lewis is a cunt," I said to him in Italian. "Perugia."

"Si?" Danny said to him.

"Si!" he said.

"How can he run when he can't speak English?" Allen asked.

"He also speaks German and Dutch."

"How wonderful," Lewis said.

His eyes were so small they seemed to disappear altogether into his face when he smiled. They were like a pig's eyes. Seeming so alert but filled with an inhuman sort of intelligence, a kind of trapped maliciousness. Those eyes made him look as though he would have eaten human flesh if it were thrown to him as slop.

"How's it going, Allen?"

"Oh, fine."

Lewis looked irritated suddenly. "What are you doing out here so early? It's supposed to be a really small train."

"Dimitri put us on," I told him.

"He's the one with the stutter, right?" Allen said grinning.

"Right." I lit another cigarette.

"They are frightening," Danny said in Italian.

"This is nothing," I assured him.

"Giovani wants to know if you would like a beer," I said to them. "I told him it was too early; would you like one though?"

"No thanks," they said in unison.

"This reminds me of when I was going to high school in France,"

Lewis said. "We lived in France for a few years? Because my dad got transferred there? Anyway, we would skip school and go out to the cafes early in the day? And eat croissant? and drink—get this—beer! We'd play quarters? God it was so funny. There we were in France? Playing quarters? In the morning?"

"Oh Lewis, haven't we heard that story?" Allen sighed. "I really want to know if Maya's okay"

"There's nothing to know," I said. "I'm fine."

"Yes Maya, but Jezz is dead." He studied my face for the slightest reaction, digging for any sign of distress. Lewis winked at him from across the table. I tried to shrug.

Danny got up abruptly and went into the cafe. I could see him flipping through a rack of postcards, taking his time before ordering.

Allen tried to refine his approach. His voice full of understanding. "You know Maya, there are people saying that his death was...." He paused and attempted to look pained from having to tell me. "Well, you know what he was involved with. You know the risks...." Lewis nodded and tried to put his hand on mine but I reached quickly for a cigarette. They were really going for it this time. The drama. The intrigue. They were on TV; *Sixty Minutes*; make up and soft back lighting; giving the sad inside story; the human face; telling about the tragic end of their close personal friend, Jezz Lethe, public school scholar turned trafficker. What a fucking joke.

I stared at Allen. Lit my cigarette.

"Boo hoo," I said. "Boo hoo hoo."

They contorted their faces to mimic worry. And Lewis actually made his tiny eyes well up with fat tears that appeared so suddenly it seemed like they had been placed there with an eyedropper.

"I heard that he was selling passports," Allen said.

I rested my head on the back of the chair and closed my eyes. Danny came back with our drinks.

"Grazie," I told him.

"Prego."

We touched bottles and drank them steadily down. I went and bought the Athens Times, which was printed in English, and sat down to read it.

Lewis and Allen made loud small talk with each other. They were so well matched and so unconcerned with one another, as if each of them now had some private performance to carry out, using the other as a prop. We sat with them until we heard the call for our train, then Danny and I ran for the platform.

"I'll take the front," Danny said. "See you in the bar."

We stepped up on opposite sides of the train which was barely full and walked down the aisles handing out leaflets. I stopped in front of a group of women with small packs. Three hundred drachmas commission. They had a map of Greece spread out across their laps.

"Hi," I said. "Where are you coming from?"

They looked up. They all had dark wavy hair and dark eyes. They may have been sisters

"Parla Italliano?" I asked.

They laughed. "No!" said the woman closest to me.

I smiled. "Do you have a place to stay in Athens?"

"Not yet." They were all staring up at me with their brown eyes.

I handed them a leaflet. "Where are you coming from?" I tried again.

"We've been touring Italy. Mostly the Venito region, but we came down south for a while and crossed at Brindisi."

"Nice," I said. "Where are you from back in the states?"

"Chicago," said the same women. The other two had gone back to plotting points on the map.

"I've been in Venito quite a bit but never Chicago," I said. "Did you spend much time in Venice?"

"Not enough! This is our first trip to Europe, and it's weird how when you look at the pictures in books you go 'oh, that's pretty, or wow, that's a cool painting,' but you really have no idea what it looks like. When you're there you can't even think. I seen pictures of the Ponta Vecchio, or, y'know, the gondolas in Venice. They can't take pictures of these things. There's no way to reproduce them. You know, do them justice." She talked with her hands. She raised her eyebrows. She smiled wide and her teeth were white, surrounded by bright red lipstick lips.

"I agree," I said. "It's all 3-D and you can walk around in it. Did you buy any glass?"

"Just a couple a beads, I couldn't afford nothing else." She rummaged through her zipper pouch and produced a small paper bag with a paisley design on it, and spilled out two delicate glass beads. They were luminous, blue and green. They came from another country, someone had made them. She already loved them. "I'm gonna get a string for them when I get home," she said.

"I had some kind of like these," I told her. "Except they were the long more squarish kind. My brother was stationed in Vicenza for a little while and he sent them to me."

She looked me over, like she was seeing me for the first time and I think she had just figured out I was American. She looked down at the leaflet. "So, is this your job?"

"Yeah."

"Have you been traveling long?" she asked, sliding the beads back into the shiny paper bag.

"A little while."

She opened the leaflet, and looked at the pictures inside of some hotel I'd never seen. This was their vacation and everything was beautiful and new. "So, should we really stay here?" she asked.

One of her friends was looking out the window. The other had her head buried in the map.

"No," I said. "Not really."

I finished the rest of the run quickly and sat in the bar smoking and waiting and going over the want ads in the Athens Times. Sometimes people took out ads looking for tourists to watch their homes or feed their dogs for the summer, in Athens or on the Islands. I was hoping to come across one of those when Danny walked in.

"We should have at least six coming back with us," he said. "Christ man, how long have those freaks lived here?"

"Allen and Lewis? Maybe a year."

"What the fuck?"

"I have no ffucking idea," I said. "Lewis' parents send him money to travel. He's clearly nuts. He looks at running as a real job. I don't think he's ever had a real job, maybe he likes it. And Allen changes his story so much it's ridiculous. He's gone from saying he was 'dirt poor.' He actually kept saying it—'dirt poor'—who talks like that? Anyway 'dirt poor' working in a factory, to saying he was in with some cocaine cartel in South America. I mean look at him."

Danny was laughing.
"Really man, you saw how awful they were."
"Fuck em. Don't let it get to you," he said.
"I hate liars," I said.
"Everyone hates liars; don't let it get to you."
"I was surprised to see them, that's all. I knew they'd do that...I knew they'd talk about Jezz." The two of them were like some parallel universe version of Jezz and Jack. The evil American Jezz and Jack. Repressed, lazy queers that didn't read and didn't drink enough. And they were malicious, whereas my friends were clever. I couldn't believe they brought up passports. Either they were fishing or it was common knowledge.
"I wish I'd met him," Danny said.
"Jezz?" I nodded. "Yeah. He was funny. He'd been everywhere, and he could remember good stories about where he had traveled, I can never remember anything. And Jack, oh man, Jack, he was the luckiest man on earth. He could talk to anyone, and he could learn languages really fast.
"Where was he from?"
"Manchester. He was a fighter, a real one not like Spero. He broke this guy's jaw one night at Paradise, cause the guy told him to stop dancing with some girl. Really fucked the guy up, knocked him out cold and went right back to dancing. But he was a gentle guy really."
Danny laughed. I wasn't sure why.
"You would have liked them," I said. They'd never get pissed off about Allen and Lewis or any of it. They'd be laughing. They saw this stuff for what it really was. "They were always making plans," I said. "Completely impossible plans. Like, here's one, like...we move to Prague and open a piano bar, so Jezz can drink and play piano and live where Kafka did."
"And what would you do?" Danny asked.
"What? Anyway, Prague is done. If Jezz and Jack were still around they'd probably want to go to Russia." I pictured the three of us in furry coats standing by a frozen river, warming our hands with boiled potatoes. "Yeah." I couldn't stop talking about them. Couldn't make myself. It was horrible. As if the only life they had, any of us had, was inside my head. And the images were so silly. I might as well have

told Danny that we'd planned on carrying out a bombing mission and then moving our G-force team to an undisclosed location beneath the ocean floor. It was just as likely as anything else we'd come up with.

"Jezz was always reading," I told him, "this horrible heavy shit like Pushkin and Tolstoy. Drunk off his ass, sweating and reading, stopping to tell us why it was so good. And Jack wrote poetry, it wasn't bad actually, and Jezz would sing these poems to piss him off! He'd set these poems to the tunes of colonial songs, really insulting stuff, like 'Marching to Pretoria.'" I laughed then, thinking about it. "For Christ's sake, it was so fucking funny, or 'Drill ye Terriers Drill.' You know that one? It's about making the Irish work harder in the mines. Or the national anthem, y'know 'God Save the Queen,' that would really get him. You shoulda heard him singing those poems." I laughed.

"What did they do back in England?"

"Jezz went to a conservatory. He got in when he was eleven. That's all he ever did. He left England one night after the pub closed. Just walked out and started hitch hiking. And that was it. Jack boxed and I guess he wrote or tried to write. He'd dropped out of school. He lived with his mother. I guess they both started traveling when they were pretty young, sixteen or seventeen or so. When I met them they hadn't been home in years. This would of be the third year for Jezz. Jack, I bet, is in the Middle East. He talked about going there all the time."

I shut up finally, to my great relief. And then just sat there feeling stupid. What would we be doing if we'd stayed in schools or had any training or done the things people do? What studies, what jobs actually appealed? Forensics? Or maybe ambulance driver, tight rope walker, fire eater, black box finder. What would we have been? Trafficker, Boxer, Vagrant, Mercenary. We had no intention of ever sitting around in well lit bohemian cafes in Prague. We'd had enough money to do that before and didn't. Prague was the lie we repeated to make us feel human. To make us forget we really were where we belonged. Each one of us had finally crossed the line into true homelessness, after having just walked it in our minds for years.

*

Night after night I wake up and there's this girl in my bed. He was standing in front of the mirror pretending I wasn't there.

Yeah? Jack asked lighting his cigarette. *What's she look like?*

A boy.

Aw, shoulda stuck with me, mate. I'm the real thing. He scratched his balls for comic effect. But he'd meant what he said.

They laughed. Jack threw a single cigarette like a dart and Jezz caught it and put it in the corner of his mouth. His hair was wet, combed back. I picked a copy of the *Athens Times* up off the floor and started reading it.

But she's mad for me, I can tell, Jezz told him. He lit another cigarette off his own and handed it to me. I smiled up at him. *She loves me,* he said. And his face broke from the act for a minute and radiated a true smile.

She's trying to take advantage of you, yeah? in your weakened state, like, Jack said. *Or maybe she's getting cold out on the balcony.*

Nah, It's gotta be my weakened state. Jezz laughed. *She likes boys who are pale yellow. 'Wanna see the lab results,' he laughed infectiously?* He grinned at his own joke.

Jack smiled. *'Give me your body,'* he said gravely. Jezz laughed. Jack looked at him. *You really are yellower,* he said. *Nothin pale about it. You look like shite these days. You know that, yeah?*

Jezz looked straight at him and drank from a little bottle of ouzo that sat at the edge of the sink. *To wicked spirits are horrible shapes assigned,* he said. Then shoved his hands deep into the pockets of his shorts and let his head roll to the side, doing his Morrissey impression. With his fake Morrisey smile. And the jaundiced melancholic pose of gay English softcore punk. He hated that he loved that music. It went against everything he'd learned in music school. And he found love neither tragic nor melancholy.

And though I may come alone, Jezz sang sarcastically. *My faith in love is still devout.*

Jack stared at him, shook his head, and Jezz laughed again. It was the manic pre-drunk hours of morning and everything was hilarious on four hours of sleep. These were the best times, the times before we had to have breakfast with David. The times when it was just the three of us.

Seriously though, Jezz sat down on the cot next to me, pulled me into his lap and tossed the comic on the floor. *Who's better looking?* He wrapped his arms around me and kissed me on the cheek. *For that matter, whose better?*

It's hard to say. Jack leaned over the bed and tied his shoes. He pulled a worn orange t-shirt over his head and then looked up. He was starting to get mad at Jezz and it showed. *Who is better at what, like?*

Who is better at it, like?

The conversation was rubbing Jack the wrong way. *I'm not here for your cock,* he said.

No? Jezz asked him, *Is it my radiant personality then? And where are we going today Mr. Bumfuk?*

Down to play dominos with Sterious, yeah. Drink his ouzo, listen to him call me a nigger. He laughed.

Why do you keep playing with him? I asked. *He's mean.*

He's alright, Jack said, and the tension had left his face. *He's just old, like, and he has a bad job. Besides, he's a good player. And he bought me me own set, like. His old man friends, like, they can't play for shite, yeah? We're good together. I'm like the illegitimate son he never met.*

I got up and rinsed my hair and face in the sink, walked on to the balcony to roll up my poncho liner. Jezz continued to sing from inside the room, a strange mix of half remembered love songs, his voice wavering between irony and disgust. It was silent for a moment and then he began his favorite one liners from *Fawlty Towers.* I heard Jack tell him to cut it out. I heard Jack tell him to stop it. I heard him say *you need to decide....* But couldn't make out the rest because he was whispering it. Finally he told Jezz loudly that he was acting like an idiot.

I know it! Jezz yelled, *it's all the attention!*

I walked back in and tossed the rolled up poncho liner on the bed and started getting dressed.

Jack stood in front of the door and Jezz put his arms around his neck, smiled at him, kissed him. Jack shook his head, laughed shortly through his nose. They were the same height. They looked beautiful together. Jack linked his fingers through the front loops of Jezz's cutoffs, shook his head again in a kind of resigned and annoyed disbelief. Jezz kissed him again, brought his hands around to gently hold Jack's face, and finally Jack kissed him back. It was hard not to. Jack whispered something else to him and rested his forehead on Jezz chest, and Jezz placed his long fingered hand on the back of his neck.

I went back on to the balcony and heard the door close.

Below our room cars sped by and a haze settled over the street. Jezz came out and stood beside me, spit over the rail. He pushed me part way over, then pulled me back quickly by the hips. I straightened up and leaned against him.

C'mon My, let's jump. He spun me around, grabbed my face and put his mouth over mine and blew air into my lungs. *Let me resuscitate you.* I loved his hands, his arms, his form... skinny, big boned, like a puppy, where you see the ribs but also the muscles. I pushed him away, laughed at him. I held his face in my hands and yelled down his throat. And then he kissed me like he'd kissed Jack. Again. And he bit me lightly on the tongue. His gestures were so familiar they were invisible. So familiar they were mocking.

We headed out. Jezz stopped half way down the stairs to check his pockets for an extra pack of cigarettes. Then he looked up at me vacantly. His expression unreadable, dazed; a misfired synapse. I laughed at him and his face lit. Eyes awake again with their same scrutiny. He grinned, pulled me to him, and rested his chin on top of my head. He folded me into his arms.

Our ribs pressed together through our thin shirts and I could actually feel his heart beating. Actually feel his muscle and skeleton. Feel the heat of his skin. His smell and his form relaxed me, relieved me, released me, like when ice finally numbs a bad bruise. When the cold meets the heat radiating from the hit. And you're comfortable enough to doze off. To dream.

Sterious looked up briefly from the game where he and Jack were hunched in concentration. A bottle of ouzo and two demitasse cups sat next to them on the edge of the desk. He gave us each a peppermint as we passed through the lobby. I ate mine and Jezz licked his and then threw it hard at the windshield of a passing car.

*

The train stopped at Elephsina and we looked out the window at the small group of runners lining up to get on.

"They'll be pissed when they see we've been on since Corinth," I said.

"They'll be pissed anyway," said Danny.

Then we were quiet, smoking and sitting across from each other. We heard the doors being clamped shut and then the steady sound of the train again. Headed for Athens.

*

They used one! He folded up the paper and went to get two more pints. A movie staring James Caan and Loretta Switt was playing on the big TV. There was a car chase and now James Caan had cornered a transvestite in the women's room of a sports stadium.

They used one, Jezz said again. *They bloody used one already!*

I took the pint from him.

Sixteen people! he said. *Jesus.*

The transvestite leapt out from behind a stall and kicked James Caan in the face.

What did you think was going to happen? I asked, even though I hadn't thought anything would happen at all.

I thought they'd sell them to someone else. I thought they just kept getting passed from hand to hand. Or maybe someone just needed them to travel. I didn't think it was this bloody efficient...this bloody.... He laughed, *This ah...ah...* He knocked back his Amstel.

I shrugged, went up to get two more pints. I looked back at him as I waited for the bartender to put up the drinks. Jezz's nose was all taped up and his face was badly bruised. And it made it look like there was something wrong with his eyes. He sat still watching the movie, breathing slowly with his mouth open and the tip of his tongue pressed against one of his incisors. We were drinking nervously, at an accelerated pace, two for every one we'd normally drink. And he paid for all of it with the money from the sale. He took another beer from me. He was neither pleased nor repentant, just startled at the speed of the trade. And a little excited. I wished I wasn't with him. I wished I had stayed back at the hotel to drink ouzo with Jack and Sterious and watch them play dominos. I wished we hadn't got the paper. I wished I didn't know anything.

Jezz kept shaking his head and pushing the article towards me.

Jens Christensen, not the olive skinned Dane who probably had his passport reissued within days of its theft from Olympos. But a Jordanian, educated in London, detained at customs in Athens before boarding a flight to Tel Aviv. Jens Christensen was detained long enough to kill twelve ticket holders, three airline employees and himself with a homemade syntec explosive in his carry-on. Jens Christensen was funded by some organization and supported by another. He represented the interests of some group. This group advocated the killing of people for ideological reasons. The paper said it was a vast network with satellites in other countries. Jens Christensen, or whatever his name was, had been trained by this group.

I just stopped reading. There were four more passports floating out there. We knew it but they didn't. Whoever the fuck *they* even were. Interesting that we could read something in the news and know the circumstances that set the event into motion. Interesting that we wouldn't tell anyone about the other false passports not even now. Jezz set his empty down and smiled. It was his only true achievement outside of taking second place for composition when he was twelve and the Royal Academy of Music competed in Warsaw.

Fuck, he said. And his speech was already starting to slur. I leaned over my mug and a single drop of blood slid from my nose into the beer. Jezz reached out with the bottom of his t-shirt and held it under my nostrils. I bled and looked at him, felt his hand beneath the shirt. He wiped my face and mouth with it, and then leaned in, kissed me. Licked the blood off my upper lip. Then he sat back.

FFFuck, he said again.

We should leave now.

He shook his head. *In a few weeks,* he said.

He went to get more beer. Came back and put his arm around me. They were dead. The people listed in the paper. The people who had been waiting. Just waiting. They were really dead. I didn't want to see him again. Not for a while. I'd tell Jack. He'd be okay with Jack. They'd be happy, say that someone else would have sold the papers anyway. What did it matter if it was one of us? If one of us finally got some money. Now we can get somewhere they'd say. They'd lie. No. Jack wouldn't lie, but he'd be more patient than me. He'd wait. Now we can go, he'd say. But he'd wait.

I watched Jezz as he watched television. James Caan's partner was putting his gun away. His eyes welled up, but he was cool and said nothing. He just squinted as the ambulance drove past. The camera pans back, rises above the crowd and the credits roll. Grainy celluloid, then fade to black.

I looked out the front windows of the bar while the last of the credits played on the screen. It was afternoon in the red light district. No one walked by, the streets were vacant. They were dead, all those people, the ones who know thousand-year-old dances. They were dead and it was time to go. Time to go again.

10

"Hello Olympos!" screamed Stephan bursting through the door of the bar. "Shitty train! Hello Danny"

"Are you drunk?" I asked, pretending to be shocked.

"Yes, yes, yes and I killed this shitty train motivated solely by the desire to take commission from that fag and his fat boyfriend."

"Your English is much better when you are drunk."

"Right," he said, leaning heavily on my seat. "We've got free breakfast," he confided in us thickly.

The hostel he worked for had no kitchen and only fifteen beds.

"Here, sit down," Danny said, directing him into the seat next to me.

"Where's David?"

"Just waking up I'd guess. We saw some dancing last night."

"Where, Popodopolous?"

"Yep."

"I saw three ghosts yesterday," Stephan said.

Danny looked at me incredulously.

"Uhuh," I said.

"I saw my Dad, Melinda, and Buddy Holly. Buddy Holly said he was really pissed off cause he wasn't in rock and roll heaven. So now I know there's a rock and roll heaven."

"I knew it," said Danny.

"Yeah. That's so, man," said Stephan, nodding emphatically. "That's so. I have something to tell you, My."

"Yeah? What did Melinda say?"

"Ah, I can't remember. She might have just been the contact for Buddy Holly. Ghosts do that."

"Umhm," I said. "Who else is running the train?"

"A few people. Me. You guys. Those pricks. And the other pricks from up town. It's a shitty train. But I killed it. I killed it. Oh, fuck, but I have to tell you...." He looked up and breathed heavily out of his nostrils but didn't say anything more.

Stephan had long blond hair, a little goatee and too much jewelry. He talked faster when he was drunk and looked haggard. His age was indiscernible. Frozen in the junkie time warp somewhere between twenty-five and forty. His face was very tan and lines radiated out from his eyes, touching his temples. He had brilliant green yellow eyes, really a rich kind of color not made for eyes at all. His teeth were crooked and his incisors stuck out slightly.

"What hotel do you run for again?" Danny asked him.

He looked up. Smiled. "Heartbreak Hotel!" he yelled, laughing uproariously. "Heartbreak Hotel Athens! Ha! Heartbreak Hotel Athens." He laughed harder and harder, shaking Danny by the shoulders, and wiping tears from his eyes. We were getting tired of the laughing, And it wasn't all that funny. But just then he broke into real sobs, choking and laughing and weeping. "Oh, I have to tell you," he said again, his voice cracked. The cries came from deep within his chest, wet and syphilitic. His body shook, he covered his face with his hands and put his head on his knees, weeping loudly and sucking air into his lungs with great painful gasps. Then he started speaking Dutch.

He slapped himself in the forehead. "He was just fucking crazy," he said. "It's not my thing to know what goes on anyway. Look at myself here. I mean look at me I actually in fact run for Heartbreak Hotel. It's true." He made a sorrowful high pitched noise. Then he slumped over, still crying and taking shaky breaths. I did not want to know what he was talking about. I wanted a drink and I wanted him to feel better and that was all.

I lit a cigarette and tried to hand it to him, but he was unable to hold it. I handed it to Danny and he took a few drags. I patted Stephan's back.

"Hey," I said into his ear. "Hey, you know what?" I said, "Jesus fuck. You don't really run for Heartbreak Hotel."

He laughed a little and continued to sob. I took out another cigarette and put it in his hand, this time he sat up and put it in his mouth, looking at the floor and wiping his eyes occasionally, and coughing. I lit it for him. "I have to tell you," he said. And then he didn't say a thing to us for the rest of the ride, just stared ahead smoking. Danny looked at me. When the train pulled into Larissis, we roused Stephan to his feet and headed for the platform.

"Olympos!" Danny shouted holding his leaflets over his head and pacing the floor. I mingled with groups of backpackers, asking if they needed a place to stay. Someone actually asked me if we took Visa and I told them to get a cab to the Plaka. I managed to talk a few Germans into coming back, and we found Danny and three other tourists and headed for the Hotel. Our commission had been traveling for days and were exhausted. They didn't care how much the rooms were, as long as they were close.

"Two-fifty for each of us," said Danny, as we walked across the busy street.

"Not bad."

"Did you see Stephan on the platform?"

"He's okay," I said.

*

You're okay, Bone. It's just a little pull.

Okay. I can't do anymore.

Don't you want to be immortal Achilles? Just ten more.

I can't. I'm done and you can't make me.

Yes, he said. *I sure can. You're done when I tell you. But eventually, if you keep doing the goddamn fucking push ups, I won't be able to make you do things. Alright? So drop back fucking down and finish your set. You hear me, My? I don't want anyone to treat you the way I do. So just fucking do them. You hear me?*

I don't want to live here, I said. *I want to go home.*

Yeah? he asked. He shook his head and released a short tense breath, *where's that?*

*

We led the tourists up the steps of Olympos and watched Sterious force a smile on to his usually stern face.

"A triple and a double," Danny said.

"Very good," said Sterious, taking two keys from their hooks and placing them on the desk. He took their money and nodded. "The second floor," he said.

Danny ran upstairs followed by five tired bodies dragging their stupid fucking backpacks.

"Why are you running the morning train?" Sterious asked.

"Dimitri put us on."

"You have also the 309."

"I know."

"What is this of your hair? Where has it gone?"

"I cut it."

He shook his head. "Dimitri," he spat. "Dimitri is a bad man."

Danny came back down, and Sterious turned on his electric coffee pot and sat down in his chair. He pulled a small string of beads out of his pocket and counted them over and over with his fingers while he spoke.

"Dimitri is so disorganized. I run this hotel by myself. I do everything. He loses passports."

"He's a flag expert, though," said Danny.

"Ha. Yes you see what goes on in his fat head."

"Why doesn't he get fired?" I asked.

He scowled and turned around to get the glasses and lift the pot from where it stood by his chair. "You know what he calls me?" He paused and we waited. "Frankenstein."

"You mean Fr-fr-frankenstein."

His face cracked into a big smile. "Yes," he said, pouring our coffee. He handed us the glasses and hummed a little. "Okay. Five hundred drachmas for you," he said after he had drunk his shot. He reached into a drawer and took out the money. "You split it yourselves, I have no change." He threw the bill at Danny who pocketed it. "I don't like this hair," he said to me. "This hair is really bad."

"Maybe you should stop combing the sides over the bald spot," I told him.

He flushed visibly. "Hey! You don't make fun of a old man's hair. It's your hair is the problem. With it not being there! My hair is old man hair! Old man hair is fine!"

"Oh-kay, Jesus."

"Now you got to grow more hair! Why you have shaved your head? You are a Jew now?"

"What?"

"I know all about it."

"The hell you do," I told him. "I got a haircut!"

He held his palms in front of his face and closed his eyes.

11

I needed some money so I could get the fuck out of Athens but here I was drinking away what I had just made. Here I was sitting in front of the Drinks Time TV again. And I could not get drunk fast enough. I needed to stop for at least two good reasons that were harder to keep straight with every drink I drank. I felt like diving through the front window of the bar, so I held on to the lower rungs of the chair in case I tried to do it. I might. Well if I did I did, there wasn't much I could do about it, was there? I had goose bumps on my arms and neck and I must have had a ridiculous grin on my face when Danny came back with more drinks. I needed to run.

"What?" he asked.

"Nothing."

He gave me my beer and put down a bottle of Ouzo 10 and a shot glass.

I watched him pour himself a shot, knock it back and shudder. I wondered why he was drinking so heavily. He was working hard at it.

And it wasn't his calling.

"What's with the fucking face?" he asked me.

I watched Danny watch television. He smiled to himself. He drank a third shot, poured it down his throat, clenched his jaw and sucked air through his teeth. I needed to run.

I lit a cigarette. I really needed to run. I fucking hated television. I had to get out of there. We'd be giving each other jailhouse tattoos next...whittling, darning our socks...trading matches for paper clips, using cigarettes for currency. In America if you go to jail they make you watch television, or they make you watch other people watch television.

"I'm going for a run," I told him.

"You've had five fucking beers," Danny slurred. He reached out and held my wrist. I shook it off abruptly. "Where's your fucking sneakers?" he asked. "Its one hundred fucking degrees out there." I left.

I walked through side streets to the great reproduction of Winged Victory at Omonia square. There it was, some headless angel god thing, in the middle of a rotary with cars speeding round it, encircling it. It seemed to be made of rust. It had been eroded by acid rain, and bleached thin from the sun. It was surrounded by undernourished shrubs and hedges. It stood armless, headless, just wings and breasts and legs. Incredibly familiar. I crossed the rotary with drunken fearlessness, and slipped through the hedge.

On the other side the square concrete base of the statue was littered with bottles, cigarette butts, newspapers and take out containers. You couldn't see the traffic from behind the yellowed greenery. But you could hear it. I was tired and I knelt down beneath the statue to retie my combat boots.

Nike, I remembered her. Victory, I recognized her. I knew her from books. She was the sister of Strength and Ambition. Hesiod wrote about them, he wrote "they have no home no resting place or road, except where god has guided them." And so they were brought to Olympos, to live under the care of Zeus. Ah, she was so fast and so familiar, even in pieces, even in the heat and the carbon monoxide, even in the smog, in the city named for her mother.

I ran there, unseen behind the hedge. I circled her as the cars circled me, sweating, crunching glass into the dirt and asphalt. Nike.

Victory. I was not Achilles, not killer, no near-mortal dressed in drag. Inside me there was something fast and strong. And still alive.

"Mom," I whispered, covering my mouth with my hand. "Mom," I said like you would begin a story.

12

Danny was sleeping on the front steps of Olympos when I got back. Sterious was on the phone. "Quiet," he said to me, glowering, with his hand over the mouthpiece.

I went and sat outside. And smoked. When I heard Sterious hang up the phone I came in.

"Can I please have a glass of water?" I asked him.

He filled a white mug in the bathroom sink of the lobby and handed it to me. It was very cold.

"I have called police to take away vagrant who sleeps on the steps," He pointed at Danny.

"He works here," I said. "You know that. And the police have never come for any call we've made."

"You don't know things," Sterious told me, pointing emphatically at my face. "Because of how you are a child." His breath was thick with liquor, and he was concentrating hard on speaking.

"Anyway, you shouldn't call the police because they will shut us down." I went and got more water and drank.

"If they come they going to take him away."

"I don't think so," I said.

He shook his head, angrily. "I saw Nigel today," he went on. "Why is his face all of a bruise?" He leaned back on the door frame for a moment, realized he was doing it and then stood up straight with his hands clasped behind his back and his legs slightly parted.

"Fight with the drivers," I said.

"Fight eh?"

"Yeah but David was there," I told him.

"David. He's always fighting. Always a fight. With anybody. You remember when he kick Jezz in the stomach and knock him out?"

"No. He broke his arm."

"No, no. The time he kick him here in the lobby. Right here. He's always have to fight in front of someone. Cowboy, PLO, IRA. He's the Frankenstein. Always have to fight in front of someone."

"I don't remember it," I told him. Shrugged.

"Right here. Right here." He pointed just inside the lobby. "Jezz come in here with David. Too tired to run so I make him a coffee. Right here," he pointed again. "Remember? and then he puts his mouth on the cup and David turn and kick him. Broke my Turkish cup. And Jezz he's out like that. Boom." He clapped his hands together sharply. "It's spot right here. He's the Frankenstein."

"What the hell are you talking about?"

"I say to him 'why do it? eh? I'm not cleaning no coffee.' Then David he pick him up to the room. Stay with him all week. The hot week. Before his parents come. You remember? I go up once some day later to bring him a coffee but he's sleeping with a pillow on his face. You remember? eh? You were in Palestine still? David laughed at me when I bring up the coffee. That Frankenstein. He's the Frankenstein." Sterious nodded, "you look up Jezz when you go home, he tells you about it."

He flipped his prayer beads over the back side of his hand and began counting them again. He was talking slowly but for some reason I couldn't anticipate his sentences and finish them in my head. If I could do that I could ignore him altogether. "You look him up again maybe you can marry him instead of some Jew boyfriend from Palestine. Or this sleeping boy the police are coming for."

I closed my eyes, shook my head. Sterious pulled out a kleenex from his pocket and put it under my nose. Blood soaked into it and soon turned it red and he handed me another one. "Put it up the nose like this." He twisted the corners of it and pushed it into my nostrils. "Jezz was good boy. He make a good husband for you, when he stop drinking. He talks about you.... He save books for you.... He have always some money. Better than that Black Jack or this American, eh? You gonna look him up?"

"Jesus Sterious, he's dead."

He raised his eyebrows. His mouth opened slightly and he breathed out a heavy stench of ouzo. I walked quickly to the bathroom in the lobby and threw up. I washed my face and held my head back to try and stop my nose from bleeding. There was a conspiracy of useless information. One stupid fact dividing into two again and again, like hydra heads. Maybe it never even happened. Maybe Sterious was just senile. My chest was tight and I couldn't breathe. Sterious was just drunk, that's all.

When I came out of the bathroom he was sitting at the reception desk. He gave me a round tin of hard candy with a picture of a pomegranate on the top.

"I know it, little Maya," he said thickly, sucking spit from the insides of his cheeks as he ate a piece of candy. "He was here for very long time." He shrugged, palms out "I just forget the bad part."

I put one of the clear red disks of sugar in my mouth and nodded. Rested my head on the reception desk. I thought about the opening montage of *Battle of the Planets.* The part where Princess is actually flying and doing a somersault in the air. And I realized then that she was Winged Victory. That my whole life I'd played at being Nike. I could see her eroding in the rotary, with wings prepared for flight. My brother told me I was Achilles. But he trained me to be Nike. To run like Nike. To cut and run.

Sterious was reading the paper now.

He lowered it and looked at me. "Jack is okay," he said. "He's not like a real nigger. He'd be better than a Jew. But you find someone quick before you look like a.... Can't go around alone like that." He pointed vaguely toward my body, pulled the kleenex out of my nose and handed me another one. Then he gave me a handful of them. "Here, put in your pockets for in case of more nosebleed."

I walked outside and sat beside Danny. No cops had come to get him. I stared at the clock across the street for a while. Ran my fingers over his sweaty hair to wake him, just to feel another person. Just to feel at all.

"Let's go," I said. "Let's get going."

13

He was panting when we reached the room. It was afternoon, and we'd had the first few rounds, then spent the morning at the Plaka.

I shook the key in the lock, twisted it, opened the door, and Jack was there in bed leaning against the wall, reading a book. Some worn out copy of *Tulips and Chimneys* Jezz had given him. His bottle of Amstel sat on the floor.

Ar'ray kids, he smiled, lay the book down.

Jezz picked me up and carried me through the door. *Married!* he shouted, and threw me towards the cot. I landed on one foot, gained my balance and laughed. Jack raised his Amstel and drank. Jezz grabbed me and kissed me. *Married!* he yelled again. He squeezed me really tight.

Stop, I told him.

Jack looked at Jezz incredulously, then shook his head and laughed, *Did yous actually get married, like?* he asked me. His face fumbled with a smile but it got away.

No, I told him.

We had the reception at Drinks Time, Jezz said. *We'd have invited you but it was very exclusive.*

Very, I said. I washed my face in the sink and dried it on the front of Jezz's shirt. I lit two cigarettes and gave him one. He held it and gave me another kiss. Then coughed for a few minutes. *Married!* he yelled, and squeezed me again too hard, crushing my arms into my sides.

Stop it, I said.

Marriage is a sacred institution, he said in a serious tone.

He sat down on the edge of the bed and took his shirt off. I unlaced my boots.

We all three on the 309?

Yeah, said Jack. *Yous want to go out for a bite first? Go for a walk uptown, like. I've got a mate busking outside of Argos, plays beautiful guitar, yeah?*

I'd love to but I made plans to fuck my wife. You see we are now forever bonded, and so must consummate our betrothal without additional companions.

Jack looked away, shook his head. *Right then, I'll be playin dominos for a bit.* He got up and put his shorts on over his boxers. Washed his face and ran a soapy finger over his teeth. Put on a t-shirt and his rubber sandals. Then stood in front of our bed. *Ar'ray,* he said, then waited. *Ar'ray. I'll.* He kept pausing, standing there. *I'll be up after nap time.* And he leaned down and kissed both of us in turn. *Congratulations,* he said to me. *You must be very proud.*

As soon as he left Jezz dug the rest of the pints out from under his bed. There were eight bottles. He opened two with his teeth and we drank them and took off our sweaty clothes.

Why'd you tell him no? He asked me. *Why'd you tell him no when he asked if it was true?*

I shrugged. I lay down beside him and rested my head on his ribs. I put my arm around him. Put my leg over his waist and closed my eyes. He ran his hand through my hair. Put his lips against my forehead.

Why?

Shhhh.

He was quiet for a while.

Let's go to Morocco, he said.

Okay.

Let's go to Israel and then Egypt and then Morocco.

Okay.

How much money do you have?

Forty bucks, I said.

What's that?

Eighteen pounds.

He moved down and kissed me on the mouth. Scratched his fingers lightly over my skin. He tasted like cigarettes. *Let's go to Prague then,* he said.

Okay.

Unless we get more money. There's got to be a way to get more money.

I nodded. Lay beside him.

He pulled me closer to him. Wrapped me up in his long arms, breathed deeply, curled beside me and reached down to rub my pubic hair. He pulled it up gently, straightening it out, letting it curl again. He smiled with those beautiful lips. A content smile. It welled in the chest and spread to the face, this look of his. *Open to me my sister,* he said. *My love, my dove, my undefiled.* He kissed me and let his palm rest. And his smile became a laugh. *I want to find your little cock,* he said. *I know its here somewhere.*

I pressed his face down. *Look for it.*

He searched with his fingers. *But where is it?* he whispered. I could feel his breath on me. *Where is your little cock? Mmm? Ah, ah wait, there it is,* he sang, pinching gently. *Mm. Must suck your little cock, Princess.* He put his warm mouth over me and I curved my face into him, pressed against his chest, reached down to pull myself through his thighs, to hold his penis, pinch the head gently and slide my finger along the tiny keyhole till it grew wet.

There it is, I told him. *There's your little puss.* He laughed and lapped at me. I pushed forward and filled my mouth.

A perfect calm had descended upon us, a preverbal world. He sucked me, and then slid his smooth body along mine in this sea of blindness and peripheral vision. His skin grew flush in patches. And I righted myself to look at his face. I watched the smile spread from his body to his mouth. And then felt it spread onto my mouth into my body. There was no calm as complete as this. No waiting. No leaving.

This was the place I could stay, the only place not corrupted. And in it I could see stretches of time. Minutes, months, years worth of time, that ran like ribbons that shone solid and vibrant, inside his blue eye. I could see it. The eye that was lodged in the face, in front of the brain of Jezz. This was the promise of relief. And the urgency to get there was hard wired.

And everything slowed down. Moved at its proper pace. Each gesture was taken as precisely as it was offered. A drunken machine of pores and tiny hairs, of nerves and blood. Smell and taste overwhelmed, flooded the heart and pushed it along. All the distracting stimuli, all the sight and sound and strain of speaking had finally folded in on itself. That's what it was like inside his eye, on the surface of his skin, in the darkness of his viscera.

His hair line was beaded with sweat which ran down the sides of his face. He was all limbs and bones. We were like insects.... Wasps waists.... So very little separated our insides from outside. And again the heart's beat could be felt through the warm skin...through the cage that held it in. And our mouths were wide dark holes in our skulls, beautiful echoing churches where senses collapse into unity.

All the corporeal terror was erased, submerged, drowned. A new kind of animal was being born, a new kind of breathing. We are drawn into one another's eyes, filtered through them, and replaced with our true selves. We smile at one another, ah we are equal, contained in this skin. We are identical, pressing to get out of it. And now there is no more waiting.

He closed his eyes tightly and his mouth opened gently then wider as he took a deep breath, held it, and let it out in short laughs. Then we sat with our backs against the cool wall.

Oh god. It's a dream, he said. *It really is.*

Mmmm.

Pass me a beer, Princess.

I opened one and drank, then handed it to him and he drank the rest of it. The shadow of the balcony door descend the wall. It lay across the bed cutting us down the middle with a gray line. Orange squares of light shone on our chests, while the sweat dried.

Why'd you tell him no we didn't? he asked. *Jack, I mean.*

I held his hand, looked at the darkening ceiling.

Seriously, I just wanna know s'all. Hm? My? My? Maya? Answer me, My. Why'd you tell him no? Why'd you....

14

"The two of you look like hell."

Danny and I looked at each other. He really did look like shit. Much worse than he had a few days ago. David stood with us at the station kiosk where we were buying cigarettes and he was buying cookies.

"We didn't get any sleep," I told him.

"At least you've made up for it by drinking all afternoon." He waited for me to light a cigarette before telling me to put it out.

I threw it onto the platform. A tall kid in knee length khaki shorts and a fluorescent yellow tank top cut in front of David at the stand.

"Excuse me," said David, tapping him on the shoulder. "I was in front of you."

The kid looked back at us, and then turned around again, ignoring David.

"Excuse me?" David said, tapping him too gently.

This time the kid turned around and stared at David. "Don't be a wanker," he said.

David looked straight up, taking a deep breath, as if he were trying to control his temper; then with a great force propelled his forehead into the kid's nose, flattening it, splattering blood across the counter of the magazine stand in one rapid snap.

The kid grabbed his face in pain, blood was running down his yellow shirt. His eyebrows were raised and his mouth was open, filling up with blood that he eventually spit on the floor and on the front of his clothes. I don't know why he didn't close his mouth.

"Oh God," he started a panicked angry sort of crying. "You broke my fucking nose."

David smiled broadly at him. "You'll have to get that set," he said.

The kid ran into the station house holding his nose and leaving a trail of blood. No one seemed to have noticed the event except for the magazine vendor who was already wiping down the counter with a soapy towel. It happened fast. And it was very very funny, like only unexpected pain can be.

"It's never funny when you expect it," I said.

"Jesus Christ!" Danny yelled.

"No it isn't, is it?" said David to me, matter of factly, wiping a red splotch off of his forehead. He licked his fingers and rubbed again till the blood was gone.

Danny and I walked out on to the platform to sit and smoke away from David.

"Jesus!" Danny said again. Then he laughed. "Holy shit. I can't believe he just did that. That kid didn't do anything. Holy fuck man." He was getting loud and repeating himself. And he needed to let it go.

"Do you have a bottle for the train?" I asked him.

"No, but good idea," he said. He ran quickly across the platform in the direction of the station shop, returning about five minutes later with a bottle of Ouzo 10.

We watched Stephan as he told a story to a group of runners down the platform from us. He gestured wildly and they laughed. We watched taxi drivers walk across the platform swinging their keys and sticking out their chests. They'd been told once to stay off the platform. They must have been insane.

Greek music played inside the station and could be heard out on the platform, below the conversations.

"When's the train to Athens due?" some skinny runner asked us.

"We're in Athens," Danny said.

"Oh yeah," he said laughing, looking around. "Can I bum a smoke?"

I gave him a cigarette and he stood in front of us smoking.

Tom walked across the platform with the other runners from his hotel. He was wearing a tie dyed t-shirt. He had a long row of black stitches near his mouth and a purple green bruise which disturbed the continuity of his pale placid face.

We sat and watched him drink beer and fold leaflets. Tom was interesting now because his face was fucked up, he was the new reason to fight the drivers. He was the white South African tourist martyr of the Larissis train station.

I watched David. He was not doing his usual entertaining tonight. He hadn't moved from the doorway and his expression hadn't changed. He stood in his jean jacket, eating his lemon creme cookies and watching. The lines in his face seemed deeper, yet he was still ageless, tireless. I imagined he missed Jezz more than anyone. He'd spent the most time with him. Sat with him after he'd gotten hurt. He was like Jezz's big brother. He might as well have been a statue standing there, but for the light that never left his eyes. He was waiting too, idling in Athens instead of in Green Cross or Long Kesh. Jack had left, and Jezz had died, and he had only me. He had been abandoned.

I felt a sudden shock of despair run through my stomach and chest, and felt for a moment that I couldn't breathe. My eyes became wet; my body felt cold; and then it was gone like a fleeting vision from the train window. I wouldn't leave him for that long again. I wouldn't just leave him alone here. It had all been a mistake.

The train pulled slowly into the station, and we pushed once again towards the doors. Ready for the short ride, the bar car, ready to wait again and again for the next round.

15

"I love you man," Stephan said. "You are great, you are the greatest. And I love that song, it's beautiful."

Danny was sweat soaked and holding on to the side of a metal counter for support. He and Stephan had just finished several deafening choruses of "Are You Lonesome Tonight," and they were now standing unsteadily in the middle of the crowded bar car staring in each others general direction with big grins on their faces.

"Oh yeah, yeah I know. Yeah. I love that harmony," he said. "Elvis. Mmhmm. You should be in a band Stephan; you don't really belong here." He gestured around at the rest of us, still beaming into Stephan's rosy face.

I gazed out the window. I had to make some money. That was all I could think about. With what I had now, the farthest I could get was one of the Ionian islands, and it was hard to stay in those places long. Hard to find work. I put my head against the pane and my hands on the glass to shade it from reflecting the crowd behind me. I tried to look out into the dark countryside, but we may as well have been traveling under ground. There was nothing to see. Tonight we'd go to Paradise and there would still be nothing to see. Just the same group with their stories running together like one text. One dialog that we'd all learned a piece of and could say by heart. Some fragment of memory or film or rumor that somehow each of us knew, playing in a constant loop. Over the narrow strip of track that ran between Piraeus and Corinth.

Runnin the 309 again? Jezz asked, resting his hands on my shoulders. They were clammy. He was actually cold now. *Why you still here?*

"I was about to ask you the same thing. I guess that 'till death do us part' thing was bullshit."

D'you miss me?

"My god, yes. Are you kidding?"

D'you hear em singing? he asked. He was dirty and his skin had a yellowish tint to it. He brushed his hair back from his forehead with his hands. He was thinner and his elbows bulged in the middle of his arms.

"How could I miss it?"

Look there's the foundry, he rested his chin on my shoulder as we looked out the window together. The foundry lit up the countryside and for a moment I couldn't see our reflection in the window.

I just can't think why you're still here, he said quietly into my ear. His lips were wet and his breath smelled like cigarettes and mildew. *David's easy, and Mike, n'Nigel; but you and me and Jack are different aren't we?* He leaned down and brushed his face against the back of my neck, put his arms around my waist. He rested his head against mine and leaned there. Thinking. *Did you come back to tell me something? Some little secret?*

He knew that the things he said sounded good coming from a corpse, and he was happy to have me think of him as omniscient. But there was something off about him. He wasn't as quick as he used to be, back when we slept together beneath the non-existent stars. He didn't know what to say now. He looked straight into the glass at my face and held me a little tighter he felt my ribs, moved his hand across my stomach. He kissed me. *It was hot in our room after three days without a drink.*

"Don't make a big deal out of it," I told him. "It was just a few days."

Who called my parents? he asked. *Di'you?*

"No. I don't know. I don't know. Well, actually I...."

None of these people did. He looked around at them and his shoulders slumped visibly. He was getting tired of the revenant spook act. *Fuckin'ell, My. Fuck me. I'm still on this fuckin train, and I don't know a bit more then I did a month ago. Train, bar, bed, boat—all the fuckin same but wiv no money. My fuckin gut hurts and I got a headache.* He took a shaky breath. *I can't feel you that good either.* He ran his hands over my face. *You feel like you're covered in talc.* He spit on the back of my hand and rubbed vigorously. He bent over and rubbed his hollow cheek against mine. He wrapped his arms completely around me so that they crossed and met back at his shoulders. I relaxed and leaned into him.

"You need a drink, baby," I told him. "That's all."

He nodded, *too right.* He pulled me further into his chest. He was trying to pull me into his body and I wanted him to. I wanted to see if he could really do it, but he seemed too weak or exasperated to continue. He stepped back. Coughed. He actually coughed. Looked through his pockets. There was nothing in them.

You know what? Hey, You know what? All those people what got blown up? The ones that got blown up cause of.... You remember that right? They're not here. Jens Christensen, he's not fucking here. My grandfather's not here. Nobody's here. Those Costa Ricans David told us about—they're not here either. Hitler, Churchill, Sid Vicious. I haven't seen 'em. Not once. I haven't seen a fuckin soul.

He shook his head and rubbed his eye tiredly with a boney fist, I could see the tendons spread out on top of his hand. He was exhausted and looked like he might cry.

"Is Jack there?" I asked him. "Do you know where Jack is?"

He shook his head. He was so tired. I missed him terribly. I linked my finger through the belt loop of his shorts.

"I need to leave," I told him.

He looked startled and instantly less tired. *Come with me, then.*

I shook my head. "No."

Please, he said. *I'm lonely. I've got no more books now that I finished the Blake. Come here and this time I really will just think and read with you. I promise. We'll go right away, we'll pay for a flat a year in advance and we'll buy bicycles. I promise, Princess. We'll drink hot sweet tea. I do, I really just want some tea now. I'm freezing. I don't want to be dead.*

"No. I know it. What happened to you, baby?"

What do you think? He sounded tired and shaky. *Fucks sake! Why are you so dumb?*

He looked at my face, *Whatta ya gonna do, My? Leave me? You got that leave me look.* He leaned forward, put his mouth over mine and sucked air out of my lungs, then blew it back on my forehead. It was cool, felt so good. I held his face in my hands and looked at him. His skin was soft and bruised looking, stretched over his skull. And his eyes were deeply sunken into his head. He smiled.

"Maya?"

I turned, shocked at how close the voice was to my ear.

"Oh, Mike." His face looked different.

He held my shoulders. "Y'alright?"

"I'm fine."

"Train's in a minute."

*

In truth there was nothing that made me happier than leaving. It brings the true nature of the world within sight. Every time my brother and I would leave one base for another, my heart would swell with love and compassion. Every time we drove through a city for the last time or a countryside we would never have to see again, I would feel the need to sing. Every time we crossed out of a city, the arches of a freeway passing above our heads, the sun's reflection on the windows of buildings, we would smile at each other and I would suddenly recognize him and all the places we were passing. I would recognize the 7-11s and the gas stations and the billboards as they shot by. And the curve of his cheek and his chipped tooth, as I sat by his side. A comfort and beauty to all these things unfolded like words in a book. And there were hours and hours of quiet highway, and no school, no interruption of thought. Everything just flowed. The radio static or the songs were beautiful. The traffic or weather reports, transmitted to us via invisible bands across thin air, were beautiful.

Sometimes I read out loud to him while he drove, with the window down and the sun on my arm. I remember him switching the station and Tom Petty singing while a wheat field flew past at the edge of the black road. *You can stand me up at the gates of hell,* he sang, *but I...won't...back...down.* When it was over John said, *That's the ballad of Maya Brennan.*

Those were nice days but they were coming to an end. And those were nice words but that wasn't my song. My song was the road receding in the side view mirror. And I was happy to hear its silence again.

*

It was dark when I stepped down and turned to look at the other runners getting off the train with their last few pints for the wait. Stephan stepped down yelling and holding on to Mike's shoulders. Seconds before the train pulled away, Danny stepped out the door, missing both metal steps and landing on his hands. A cheer arose from the bench. He pulled himself up, waved at us, and staggered over to the side of the shack. He leaned against the door frame, trying to light a cigarette for several minutes and brushing gravel out of his hands.

David and Mike stood chatting. Another group nearby was reliving last night's romp through Paradise. I knew that I was very drunk and tired, but felt aware, alive at least. I looked over at Danny again. There was no way he'd make the train conscious. He squinted at me and then staggered over to sit on the bench.

"Maya," he said thickly, putting his arm around me.

"Danny, that was a lovely rendition of 'Are You Lonesome Tonight.'"

"What? Oh, wasn't it?"

"Yes."

David spotted Danny and came over, grinning sarcastically. "Now you look much better. Pepped up quite a bit the both of you. Don't let him talk to anyone on this train if you want to bring back commission," he said, squatting in front of our bench.

"I'll be okay," Danny said.

"Don't worry, we'll lay him out somewhere," I said.

"You mean you will, if there's even room. It's high season; this train will be packed."

"I'm fine, I'm fine," he said shrugging, shaking his head, and holding up his hands in some kind of miscalculated gesture of nonchalance that looked like it was making him dizzy.

David and I stared at him.

"He's fine," I said smiling.

David slapped me on the knee and stood up. "Yeah. He's fine."

"I'm okay," Danny said.

Stephan came to sit with us, he was in a beautifully manic mood. He was loving everyone, you could see it in his eyes, he had peaked and the crossed synapses were infusing everything with a sense of holiness. He was loving Danny, loving the bench, loving his leaflets. He was radiant with love. His eyes glistened and shone into mine, his chest swelled with emotion. With great delight he pulled a crumpled up piece of newspaper out of his pocket and waved it in front of me. "My! Maya, look." He waved the page around some more, rubbed it against his face and then took a bite out of it. He chewed it slowly while rubbing the rest of the paper carefully between his hands, and then over his chest like it was a bar of soap. "It's...mnnnn...for you. I told you I would tell you." He pushed the remaining tattered piece of newspaper forward, swallowing and smiling wide. I took it. He squeezed my hand and rocked back and forth, took a luxuriously deep drag on his cigarette.

"Thanks," I said. I pushed the crinkled newsprint into my back pocket and nodded at him. "That's thoughtful of you." I lit a cigarette.

"Yeah! Can you believe it? And you know what else?" he asked me earnestly. "Danny has a bastards degree!" He and Danny laughed. Then Stephan stood and grinned at me with his eyebrows raised, for longer than he should have.

"Yep. Danny's in bad shape right now, though. He's been up for days running. Maybe you could take him to the toilet and splash some cold water on him?"

"Of course I could." He grabbed Danny by the hand, and the two of them staggered off to a single stall and spigot at the back of the ticket shack. When they returned, Danny's face was dripping wet and his hair was soaked.

"I feel better," he groaned.

He slumped back down, letting his head fall back against the bench, looking straight up. After a while he pulled his head up and immediately lost balance, falling to the side and catching my arm for support. "Fuck," he said.

The train appeared while I was trying to pull Danny back onto the bench. Stephan leapt forward to greet it with great strides. Arms outstretched and head back, he stood and admired the beautiful machine, deeply satisfied, laughing and skipping in anticipation and pleasure. It was some immense mythological animal that he was praying to. He wrapped his arms around himself, shook his head back and forth. When it came to a full stop he ran forward, yanked open a door in one of the middle cars, and hopped inside, closing it quickly and locking it. Other runners would have to get on at the first and last cars which had been opened for them by the conductors. I could see Stephan's face as he stood looking out the window, beaming at us with adoration, but not letting us in his car.

"It's okay," I said, pulling Danny along, then pushing him in front of me up the steps and into the first car.

It was packed. Six or seven of us were standing in the corridor in front of a narrow sliding door, pushed up against the walls and standing on people's bags and packs. Danny leaned up against the wall with his eyes closed. We stood across from him, looking at him.

Sounds of loud talking and laughing came from the rest of the train, from overzealous drunken runners and tourists excited to be so close to Athens.

"Are you guys going to Paradise tonight?" someone asked.

"No," I said.

"How come David never goes?"

"It's not his scene," I said.

"He's so funny. Man he's a riot."

"Yep."

"Does it look like there's room in the aisle?"

"No, we'll never get through this train, should have gotten on a different car."

Just then, Danny threw up, filling the hot and tiny space with the putrid sweet smell of alcohol. "Oh, Jesus," he said, and continued to vomit on himself and a backpack that lay near his feet. We stared at him. He looked up, sick and sweating, the front of his shirt a mess.

"I feel much better," he told us.

We stood across from him, pressed up against the wall waiting for him to puke again.

"Reminds me of rugby season actually," he said, taking his shirt off. "I'm fine."

Someone slid open the door to the car, and the other runners squeezed with great difficulty through, pushing into the crowd and pressing themselves flat against the other side of the door.

I stood in the corridor opposite Danny.

"Sorry," he said, and puked again, staying hunched over with dry heaves for several minutes. "Well, I hope at least we make some commission," he said, when he could speak again, standing upright wiping his mouth, and swallowing.

"I don't think so."

I was surprised that the smell hadn't made me puke as well. I lit a cigarette and offered one to Danny, then turned to peer through the door of the car. It was a little less congested; but we were still trapped until the train pulled in.

I turned around just in time to see Danny putting his shirt on inside out.

"There," he said. "I'm going to run the train." He staggered over to the door, pushed me aside and slid it open. With a deep breath he shoved his way in, pulling it shut behind him.

He must have stood there for ten minutes waiting before he realized he had no leaflets. Then his head disappeared from view, and I could see people clear away from him, stumbling on each other and looking down in horror. I heard some screams, and some laughing.

His head appeared again, gradually, and he staggered a few steps closer to the door between us. His eyes were nearly crossed and he pressed his head on the small glass pane and leaned. His face was red and his nose was running.

I slid the door open and guided his sleepless, drunken, good intentioned body forward, shutting the door behind him.

He slid down the wall and sat between two suitcases.

"My chest is wet." He closed his eyes and covered his face and began to cry. "Maya," he wept, "I have to get out of here."

16

I have to get out of here.

C'med Maya girl, Wait. We're okay for right now. Jack was sitting on the rail of the balcony with bare feet in jeans and a sweatshirt. *Jezz'll come through, then we'll all get far away, like. Somewhere good.* I nodded, looking past him at the rain outside. It poured from the gutters. It hung in the gray sky. It saturated the concrete all around and smelled like dust.

It was morning and we were up on time. But Jezz lay heavy, sleeping on the cot near the door beneath a single purple sheet. Impossible to wake. We had slapped him and thrown water on him. We thought about hiding him under the bed but figured he'd wake up under there and start moving or talking.

There are certain windows, like. Certain situations we got to take advantage of, Jack said. *We can't cut out in the morning especially, like. And not right now, not today.* He was speaking quietly, so I stood and moved closer to him. *I'm bloody sick a this as well, fairy, It's wrong I know,* he practically whispered. *But we need to leave together because...* He said a few more things that I didn't hear, then he said them again, louder, holding my face directly in front of his because he could tell I wasn't listening, but I forgot the words as they passed through his lips. I looked right at him and didn't retain a thing he'd said.

I stood on the balcony smoking. Waiting. We watched Jezz sleep, hoping he'd wake up in time, but he didn't.

David opened the door and smiled at us, up and already dressed. His face didn't falter when he saw that Jezz was still asleep. He just kept smiling at us, threw us a package of cookies and told us to put out the cigarettes. And we were glad he was in a good mood.

Did you try to wake him? Jack and I nodded. *Of course you did. But there he is just the same. What are our options?* he asked.

Let's leave him alone and go out for a bite, I said.

David sucked his teeth, shook his head. *Well, lass, we can't exactly leave him can we? We don't leave our squad.* He pushed back one of Jezz's eyelids and watched the pupil constrict. *Ah, whiskey, you're the devil,* he said sarcastically, lifting Jezz's arm and letting it flop back down on his chest. *Did you try splashing him with water?*

We nodded, less nervous, as he seemed genuinely concerned. We were now leaning by the bed eating cookies. David stood by the side of the cot with his hands on his hips surveying the situation. I wanted to be asleep too. I wanted to get out and go for a walk, drink ice coffee. Get on the train and keep going. Wait for that new landscape to appear, that can only appear fully to you when you are alone. Slide through customs and out the door into sunshine and some unintelligible culture. Not even be able to ask for the time. Not even know the word for water.

Ah well, I'll give it one more try, David unzipped his jeans and flipped his penis over the top of his underwear. *If it doesn't work we'll just have to wait here till he rises.* He grinned, straightened his shoulders, raised his eyebrows and looked up. *I'll give him another thirty seconds or so, shall I?* he asked, bouncing it on the top of his briefs. *Nah, fuck it.*

He began to piss on Jezz's chest. It splashed against his skin, like rain on dry earth but it didn't wake him. We watched him piss on Jezz's head, in his hair and ear, laughing. Like he was watering a garden and didn't want to miss anything. Jack laughed in grim disgust through his nose, then gagged audibly. Jezz rolled over, still unconscious, and the last of it got him on the back of the neck. But still didn't wake him. David shook himself dry and zipped up his jeans.

Well? That's the best I can do for now. We'll just have to wait. He laughed some more and then shot a disappointed look at Jack. *Don't bother lighting that fag, my man, you'll just have to put it out,* he said, and then sat down humming and looking at his wrist where there was no watch. He grinned at Jack.

The cot was soaked with urine and stank. Jezz's hair was dark with it, would dry sticky while he slept. It ran down his neck and the side of his face. We had an hour of watching him dream and sweat, his lips parted and his chest rising and falling. Pale gray light from the balcony ascended the wall and hung above the beautiful Endymion, as he laughed in his sleep.

Incorruptible. Impervious to instruction.

*

My brother stood in his gray sweats, stirred the sugar in the big coffee mug. It was six in the morning and we had just come back from running. I sat at the kitchen table eating cornflakes with a fork.

Are you gonna take responsibility for him or no? he asked.

Yes.

Don't tell me yes if you're not one hundred percent on this, Bone.

Then no.

Well then don't tell me what to do with him.

I'm not. He's just so little, I bent down and picked him up with one hand. His belly was the round belly of a baby dog. Pink and sparsely covered with dark hairs. I stroked his back and pinched his loose skin. *Maybe we should keep him for a little longer.* He had black shiny eyes with dark tan tufts of eyebrows. He loved to be held. *Give him to someone after he's trained a little. Someone will want him then.*

John picked the dog up off my lap and held him over his head. *That's right puppy man! That's right little doggy boy!* He smiled up at Screwy. *You're days are numbered boy-o, yes. Oh yes. Oh yes they are.* Screwy wiggled and sneezed. Stretched his front paws out in front of him and curled his tongue. *Look at this,* John said. *He actually smiles.* He smiled at the dog and lowered him down to look in his face, eyebrows knit and his mouth a flat line. He curled Screwy in his arm like a baby and continued to drink his coffee while Screwy wiggled and snorted and waved his tail around. John hadn't docked the tail because he said it would hurt him and he looked fine with it. It was the dog's head that worried him.

Screwy was a Doberman Shepherd mix. A handsome stupid dog whose head was not growing as fast as my brother thought it should. It looked like a birth defect. But the vet said it was hard to say this soon. Screwy whined a lot and walked in circles, and to John this was a character flaw that could never be corrected. He was a sweet dog though. And his coat was still downy and not yet completely black.

Just take him back to the SPCA, I said.

John shook his head in disgust. *Listen, I took him out of there. Are you going to keep him? Are you going to take care of him?*

I don't know.

Why can't you commit to taking care of him?

Because. I never asked for a dog. I looked at Screwy's little head. John carried the pup's bowl to the refrigerator and poured milk over the dry food. Then he set the bowl down and sat on the floor next to Screwy who ate with his eyes shut tight and his ears back. The skin at the sides of his face wrinkled.

John finished his coffee. Petted the dog's coat. *Yes or no, Bone.*

No. I said.

Okay.

He brought his coffee mug down full force on the base of Screwy's head. It made a loud hollow popping sound and shattered the cup. Screwy fell where he was eating, completely limp as if he were asleep.

I screamed. Stood up knocking the chair over.

John looked up at me, laughed, covered his face with his hands and shook his head for a while. He picked up Screwy's body. He cradled it, petted it some more. A small trickle of blood ran out of the pup's nose.

Oh no, he said woodenly, pausing slightly between words as if he were reading lines from a cue card. *I. Think. He's...dead.* Then he raised his eyebrows, made an exaggerated frown and pretended to blink away tears.

Fucking...God DAMN it. I'd have.... Fucking Christ! Jesus fucking Christ's sake! Why the.... What the FUCK did you do that for? I picked up the chair and pushed it in. *Goddamn it.* The dog lay completely limp in his arms. *Goddamn it....* I took my bowl to the sink and washed it and wiped the table with a sponge. It was incredible how still Screwy's body was. I looked at him. His pitiful back paws spread out on John's lap.

I'd have taken care of him, I said.

Oh, okay, he said. *Here.* And he held the body out to me.

I smirked and nodded. *Fuck you.*

John laughed *That's fuck you, Sir.*

17

The boat cut through the Aegean in white foamy crests and the air rushed into our lungs before we could breathe it, thick with salt. Our skin felt powdery and wet. We had to squint at each other under the midday sun that blazed on our shoulders. The sea sucked the heat away and the wind surrounded us, blew through our clothes, our hair, made our eyes water. We were chilled but warm inside. Dolphins leaped and arced at the side of the boat like living rubber toys closing in on us and then passing by. They looked gray and I thought they should have been blue.

We hadn't spoken much, except for Danny shouting "Oh my God!" repeatedly at the dolphins. He wandered restlessly around the boat, looking out for any sight of land. After a few hours he came and sat next to me with his feet dangling over the side of the lower rail.

"What's the plan?" he asked. "Let's plan."

"Okay, we have...like... one thousand, two, three.... Like three thousand drachmas between us which is...twenty bucks! which means we can't go back once we're there."

"Good, that should last a few days if we stretch it. We don't have to worry about where to sleep cause there's plenty of beach," he said.

"Exactly. And you have the espresso maker."

"So I guess that's the plan."

"I guess," I said. I pulled a bottle of water from my bag and handed it to Danny.

He reached into the top of his pack, and pulled out a small round watermelon. It was perfectly round with dark green speckles and stripes. He took out his Swiss Army knife, and with the long blade he stabbed the melon. It began to split as the knife sank into it, and juice ran down the side of it onto the painted metal deck. He made a few more cuts and then broke it in half. The inside was pink with small black and white seeds. He cut it into crooked wedges and handed me one.

We ate the entire melon and most of the seeds, while watching the water.

"Someone told me that on the islands your eyes change. The color is supposed to get more vibrant."

We looked at each other's eyes. "That doesn't make sense," he said.

"No. I know."

"Hey, this is where Odysseus sailed," he said.

"I went to Ithaca last year. That's where the Cave of the Nymphs."

"What's it like?"

"A cave, no nymphs."

"Too bad."

"Yeah. Paros is good though, I'm glad we're going to Paros."

"Where else have you been?"

"Ios, Ithaca, Rhodes, and Cypress, and Crete."

"What was the best?"

"Ithaca."

He smiled. We talked as if seeing everything would make things clear. We talked about people who lived on nothing all over the world, sleeping in train stations, then walking for miles to stand beneath the Sistine Chapel. We talked about these pilgrimages to nowhere. We talked about how Jezz lived in parking garages eating m&m's

for a month. How he ran out of rolling papers and tore pages out of his books to roll tobacco; the only provision he brought enough of. Danny talked about Perugia, youth hostels, art museums, and the Coliseum. We wanted to keep going. We wanted to find work and keep going.

"When do you think you'll get back to the States?" he asked.

"I can't imagine having enough money to do it," I lied.

"Get deported," he said.

"Why? What's there?"

"I guess you're right, especially after you've graduated and you realize you'll be getting the same job you would have without the degree, only now there's all the debt."

"Uhuh," I said, but I had no idea what he was talking about. It seemed completely meaningless. I didn't care about his degree or his debt, or what same kind of job he was planning on getting.

"Let's not talk about it," he said.

"Okay."

The boat was almost empty after the first stop at Ios, where about a hundred tourists, mostly German and Australian, got off.

We stretched out on the deck. I rested my cheek on the hot metal and felt my skin absorb the heat, felt my cells buzz and swarm, and the wind over my scalp moving the little hairs. It was peaceful.

18

I woke up and stared out at the sea, still lying on my stomach.

"We're here," Danny said, standing above me, his hair looked red in the sun.

I was starving. I sat up to put on my boots, They were hot inside and the soles were softer than ever, like silly putty after standing on deck with the sun pouring into them. We grabbed our packs and headed down into the hollowness of the ship and then out on to the ramp.

The port town was quiet. Only a few tourists sat in the cafe across from the docks playing cards and drinking beer. Everyone was sleeping or waiting to go to dinner, or cleaning up from the beach.

There was an immense blue domed mosque to our right, and all around us the expanse of beaches and cliffs wound their way around the island. The smell of cedar and wild sage was heavy in the air, as a constant breeze carried the odor through the tiny port town.

We stood on the brick street in front of the cafe listening to the sea roll in and out until we didn't hear it anymore. The openness of the landscape was shocking.

"Unreal," said Danny. He breathed deeply and stood looking up at the white buildings, lining the hillside with their darkened archways and blue roofs. The sun was incredibly bright, and the sea an awesome thing.

We walked past the cafe and up a hill into the center of town. It was a maze of narrow brick alleyways with small steps and archways and slopes. Grape trellises and olive trees twisted their way into the architecture, green against the cool whitewashed walls. Incense burned on a little dish outside a shop door, it was frankincense and sage. The smell drifted through the enclosed alleys and drew us to the door and darkened sleepy interior of an herb shop. Inside hundreds of narrow opaque bottles sat on shelves, elixirs for beauty, elixirs for love. Blue and white embroidered tapestries hung from the ceiling.

A little girl, maybe eleven years old, sat behind a table reading. She had a round face and black hair pulled into a pony tail on top of her head with a gold and green ribbon. Around her neck hung a blue plastic eye, set in silver. It stared out from just below her collar bone. She ignored us, chewing gum and absorbed in her book. We picked things up and put them down. Stood in the dim light under the tapestries. The girl turned the pages of her paperback. We left.

We stopped at a little grocery store with a large striped awning. Out front there was a fruit and vegetable stand, barrels of sun tan lotion, Greek flags, sunglasses, and rolled up straw beach mats. Inside, barrels of salted fish, feta cheese, and olives stood by the back counter. Cans of hummus and pickled eggplant, and calamari lined shelves that reached to the ceiling. You had to ask the grocer to use a ladder if you wanted something special from the top. The floor was cement, covered with thin carpets in Greek keys and Persian designs, and the cooler held nectars, ice coffees, and Nestle's Quik.

We bought feta, tomatoes, olives, and a loaf of bread and more water. Then we walked back down towards the cliffs, hiking about a mile then climbing up the rocky hills to a plateau covered with dead yellow grass. We had a view of the whole town and the sea which rushed at the cliffside and receded and rushed again.

Danny spread out his sleeping bag and sat down. I took out my sweater and sat down on it. The islands got cold at night. I was glad to have something warm.

"I can't believe you've been traveling this long without a sleeping bag," he said, taking out his knife.

"Mmm," I said. "I used to have a poncho liner but I left it in Israel."

Danny handed me a piece of tomato I broke up the bread, unwrapped the feta from the white deli paper. It was hard and rich and bitter. We ate like dogs without speaking for a while.

Danny got out his stove and made coffee which we drank from his travel mug staring quietly at the horizon.

Below us the town had come to life. People filled the cafes and streets and sat out on the terraces of restaurants facing the sea. We watched them from the cliff. We watched the lights come on below and headed back down before it was too dark to see our way.

We walked across the beach and heard the rising tide hissing and landing, and we saw the sea grow black. A line of cedars separated the beach from the narrow brick road. The sand was giving up the last of the day's lingering heat. All was in transition under the darkening, purple sky. All was calm and alert. Two legged creatures walked in pairs, and groups, and alone, across the vast evening beaches and roads, and under the yellow lights. Waiting for the satellites, the starry night, the bonfires, waiting to burn their silhouettes into the invisible air.

*

I don't know yet that I'm dreaming. I'm sitting in a long tiled hallway. And I'm reading. The words on the page have white paths between them. The hall is open at one end to the outside. From over my book I can see what I think is a tree and its yellow leaves are moving gently. The leaves sway and turn to one another, brush against one another. The tree moves to a little melody that I cannot hear.

When I squint, my eyes reveal the tree to be a fire. A fire, far away at the end of the hall. The flames are a kind of motion that I want for myself. A tall slow open blaze that sways like the tree's slender limbs. The fire's light is good to read by.

I don't know I'm dreaming until I hear my own steady breath and recognize it as belonging to a sleeper. Then I feel my head brush the back of the couch as I nod, yes. Yes. But my eyes are still on the page of the book. I still smell the smoke. I am reading about the tree's song. And now I need to stay asleep to finish. I needed to stay asleep to read it. This book about the tree is nowhere else, its only here. I'll never find it out there. The white paths between the words become clearer, all the little mazes standing out brightly, aglow.

Trees are really fires, the book says. This was common knowledge lost in the fifteenth century.

Books are really fires, the book says. Fires move the way you want to, listen to this melody. Can you hear it? No, the tones are produced by things that no longer exist. By insects, and those insects are extinct. The species stopped producing females. They were red and orange and blue and yellow and they stopped producing females. In the fourth century C.E. And became extinct.

The book had photographs, but now that I knew I was dreaming, I questioned their accuracy. I disbelieved the fire's glow upon the page. I could still smell the smoke but my head was nodding yes to someone. Yes. I'm up. I'm up. And now a whistle was blowing, shrill, like someone screaming. It was time to run. Or it was time to lift. Up, no more napping. My body would soon do it for me like it was trained to, but in the dream I had a little time left so I sat up and put my gummy shoes on. I buckled them up. I put my book down and ran down the hall, towards the fire, fast like Nike. I wanted to hear the victory song.

I felt instead the sun, my cheek against the sand. I could just make out part of the melody.

19

Then a whistle blew.

A voice connected to a steady pain in my ankles finally made itself clear.

"C'mon, go go," someone said, kicking my feet.

I opened my eyes and looked straight up at a cop who was continuing to kick me while looking somewhere else. His uniform was dark and he looked hot. I sat up and pulled my knees to my chest. My shirt was wet with sweat. I was thirsty and thought the cop must be too. He looked down to see that I was really getting up and then moved on to kick someone else with equal distraction. "Up up," he said to the next sleeping body.

The sun was rising and the beach was scattered with dazed tourists and vagrants, rubbing their ankles, rummaging through their packs, and rolling up their bags. I stood up and smoked, looking out at a dead calm sea. The sand was cold in the early morning light. The beach was crowded. At least twenty more people had shown up to sleep there since we had crashed. Danny rolled up his bag.

He pulled our passports out of the pack and we stuffed them into our front pockets, put on our shoes and started walking, leaving our bags under a tree at the edge of the road. The sand gave way beneath our feet and weak ankles, so we walked right at the water's edge where it was wet and firm, and we could kick the flotsam and seaweed along in front of us. We picked up the orange spikey bodies of urchins and threw them far out into the sea.

The brick terrace was covered with folding wooden chairs and small square tables meant for two people. Danny sat down and I went into the cafe. An old glass counter displayed pastries and rolls and spanikopita. Behind it was a cooler containing bottles of beer and retsina and juice. A tall man in a white button down shirt sat at a table near the counter drinking coffee. He looked up at me. His eyes were dark and he had dark circles under them.

"Can I help?" he asked.

"Two coffees, please."

"He nodded and went behind the counter. "Nescafe?"

"Yes, please."

He gave me two white mugs and I gave him some money and brought the coffee back out on to the terrace where Danny sat watching the water in a daze, his hair full of sand and sticking up all over his head. He took the coffee and sipped it making a horrible face. "It's instant."

"It's not so bad really."

He gulped the entire cup down. "I haven't felt so rested in months," he said half an hour later.

I nodded.

He looked at me for a while, a look that seemed familiar, but that I couldn't quite get. There was a sub-text. There was something I was supposed to meet or return.

"Wow, Maya, you're really tan."

"Must have been from sleeping on the boat."

"I thought people like you are supposed to burn and get more freckles."

"People like me?"

"Irish."

"Black Irish," I said. "Raped by Spaniards."

He looked at me a little longer and then back out at the sea. Then he whistled the theme music from the *Beverly Hillbillies*, as if the words 'raped by Spaniards' caused some behavioral modification glitch that forced him to whistle that song, or maybe caused some instant white trash association that translated to a childhood sitcom experience.

"When up from the ground came a bubbling crude," he sang. "Oil that is...."

I looked out at the blue sea.

"Texas tea..." he sang

Whitewashed buildings were built into the cliffside. Houses were carved into the cliffs themselves. Were joined by winding paths. So white and shadowed in the morning sun.

"Black gold...." he sang and then he just whistled the rest of the song.

A few stragglers from the beach came to sit and eat big breakfasts and use the bathroom. It was quiet. It took me several hours to finish my coffee. Mornings started late. There was the sun and no sounds of cars, already there was no sense of time. We sat until the cafe was full, then walked back to our packs on the beach.

Several people were lying in the sun and wading in the water, their bodies tanned and oiled, their faces covered with towels or their eyes hidden by dark glasses. Danny held my hand as we walked. His hands were exactly as big as mine. I could have been him. Could have been a son.

"Tonight we can walk through town," he said.

"Um hmm."

"I'd like to see the entire island."

"If we rent a motorcycle we can. It'll cost eight hundred, maybe a thousand."

He unfastened his sleeping bag from the pack and carried it down to the beach, spreading it just before the tides edge. We took off our shirts and shoes and put them under the sleeping bag.

"Serious farmer tan," he said looking at my body.

I looked at him. His chest was still pale. It seemed a physical impossibility. Only his face was burnt. I got up and ran into the waves and swam until I couldn't feel the sand under my feet. The water was warm and calm. I floated listening to myself breathe and sinking a little every time I exhaled. I closed my eyes. Water filled my ears. Hold me up now, I whispered to the sea. hold me up now. Hold me up now.

*

He was stationed in Florida. We did two sets of fifty sit ups and three sets of thirty push ups everyday at five in the morning before running to the beach. That day there was hail. Chunks of ice the size of walnuts rained out of the sky, striking the pavement and smashing to bits. We stood in the doorway of the apartment and watched. He grinned and raised his eyebrows.

Let's move out, Brennan, he said. He giggled and nodded at me and I could see his chipped bottom tooth. *Go-go-go-go-go-go-go!* We ran out the door and down the middle of the street. Our bare feet stung with impact. The air was hot and humid, and the cold hail pummeled us. John kept laughing and lifting his knees high as we ran. Every once in a while he would reach over and grab me by the arms and swing me in a circle around him, dropping me back down to run beside him again.

I felt like I could never stop running. Like I would never want to or have to. I would never tire. My ankles would never hurt again. I would never have to stop. I was five feet of steel. Our feet slapped against the wet pavement and I spread my arms out and screamed in delight.

*

Water went up my nose. I opened my eyes and dived down to touch the sand with my hands. I came up squinting at the beach and treading water. Danny was lying on the sleeping bag reflecting the sun with his white body, restless in the heat.

I swam closer to the beach and rode a wave into the shallow water, walked back to the sleeping bag and lay on my back next to him with my wet cut-offs sticking to my thighs, feeling heavy. Feeling my lungs for what they had become.

"Hey, you know what?" he asked.

"What?"

"We're going to sell watermelon on this beach." He was really excited.

"Alright."

This was the difference between Danny and Jezz. Danny's sense of his European adventure included a tightly edited scene where images of him sweating, cutting up watermelon, and exuding an irresistible charm for the sunbathers, were interspersed with images of him smiling in a haggard, self-deprecating way while he tucked wads and wads of small bills into his pockets. Eventually there would be a watermelon stand on the beach called Danny's, and Danny would have a wealthy Greek girlfriend whose father didn't approve of their relationship, and whose mother covered for the girl while she stole away to cliffside rendezvous with the handsome American.

But Jezz saw one deft maneuver, one continuous shot. He saw the dark archway above the reception office, the receptionist sleeping with the key to the safe in his breast pocket. He saw his hands steady, saw the silver key catch the light for just one brief moment, and then disappear into the darkness of his closed hand. He saw the delicate, silent act of opening the safe and removing forty official documents (mostly British and American). He saw the back of his own sleek form as it slipped into the night with a black zipper pouch, walked three blocks and swiftly passed the pouch to a man walking in the opposite direction, who in turn handed him a fat white envelope. And then he saw us reading quietly, smoking Dunhills, and listening to the Velvet Underground in the apartment in Prague.

The apartment we never smoked, or read, or sat in. In the city we never saw. Never attempted to get to.

"Alright," I said again. "Okay Watermelon Boy." I smiled at him and handed him a couple hundred wet drachmas.

Danny got up and walked towards the cedars and the road, as I lay drying in the sun and smoking.

*

We stopped running when we reached the deserted beach. The hail had already begun to turn to rain. We looked out at the ocean and sky which were the color of slate. Massive waves fought each other and shattered on the beach.

Ready? John asked.

Yeah.

We ran into the water and were immediately struck down. He grabbed my hand and we walked out farther and farther into a mass of currents and undertows and waves. The rain making thousands of expanding circles around us, perfectly round at first and then they scattered and dispersed and were swallowed. We struggled to stand under the dark sky and water. Once we started to swim it was a little better. We could ride waves or duck under them. We swam out until the crests were gone and the ocean swelled and the beach looked tiny and remote. The water lifted us hundreds of feet and then flew away again, leaving us standing out there so far, immersed only up to our chests. False calm, and then off our feet again.

I turned from the beach and looked out at the ocean which was enormous and insane and went on forever. It looked like a desert. The swells almost indistinguishable from the entire mass. The mist and fog meeting at the horizon like a distant wall, like nothing. He was laughing. John just kept on laughing. Shaved head, cleft chin, small blue eyes.

He swam to me and yelled in my ear.

Can you see where we left from? This was what he had been laughing about.

Right there, I shouted, pointing back down the shore and a little to the left.

No, he shouted. *Right there.* He pointed at a red marker on a pier that seemed miles down shore.

I hadn't noticed how fast we were being drawn away. It was amazing how disoriented I had become from trying to keep moving. He grabbed me by the back of my t-shirt and pulled me against the current and then shoved me in front of himself.

Come on Bone, he yelled. *If both of us die, won't be anyone to go to the funeral.*

We swam towards the beach in a diagonal line, propelled by a mass of deep water. The closer we got to the beach the harder it was to swim. A wall of water hit me, pushing me down hard into the sand. I scraped my forehead and lips. My neck twisted and my feet felt air for maybe a second. I drank water. I pushed at the bottom with my hands but the bottom was already gone. When I finally stood again my brother was looking back, laughing. He was laughing too hard. His eyebrows were raised, his chin sticking forward and his mouth round.

It took us half an hour to reach the shallow waves again and walk to the beach. Another hour, and more, to walk back to the apartment.

You're little, he said still laughing and breathing hard. *You are little,* he said, enunciating the t's. He smiled and took my hand, pulling me forward so I could walk next to him. My calves hurt from walking in the sand. We were going fast. And he leaned on me with his elbow digging into my shoulder. *Hold me up now, girl. You hold me up now.*

*

Danny returned with a little watermelon in a white plastic bag. He sat down next to me and began to cut it into wedges with his knife. He was concentrating, trying to get all the slices the same. I wanted a drink badly.

"How much are you going to sell it for?"

"The melon cost three hundred drachmas, so, like one hundred a slice."

"Sounds good." I ate a piece and spit the seeds into the sand.

He had fifteen or twenty slices. He put them back neatly into the plastic bag, and went down to the water to rinse off his hands. I took another piece while his back was turned and tried to shove the entire thing into my mouth, before he came back, smiling, full of some strange courageous look I couldn't place at first. Studied carelessness. Nervous and reckless at the same time. No amount of beer would really fix it, the set jaw of enduring Real Life. I could see him clearly; testing himself by hurdling bushes in his lush back yard, flexing in front of his mirror, eating in front of the TV after rugby practice. I could see his parents house, cool wallpapered in white on white, bloodless, warm in the winter. The ceramic dog food bowl with a name on it, the bookshelves. Original prints, uninspired but expertly matted. The television tastefully hidden in another room where it's always on. Favorite cereal, favorite commercial, endearing anecdotes about pets, and his father's college roommates. It was all over his body.

He wiped his hands on the front of his shirt, and ran them through his hair pushing down cow licks.

"I hope this works," he said.

"How could it not?"

He headed down the beach, stopping only to sell melon.

20

He couldn't drive. And he also wouldn't drive. Which caused me to revise my vision of his life of leisure to one that was more comfortably neurotic. But he had made enough money selling melon to rent a bike.

We sat on the cliff again, eating a late dinner and spitting olive pits into the sea. And I told him he was a genius.

"That's right. And y'see that's why I won't be renting a motorcycle, or sitting on the back of one while you drive it."

I shrugged.

"We can buy a lot of beer, how's that?"

"We can buy a lot of beer and rent a bike," I said.

He looked at me.

"Your eyes are very dark," I said.

He smiled, and something seemed to degrade immediately, change from celluloid to electronic. There was an instantaneous drop in graininess, and the quality was poor, shiny, too clearly focused. My vision became obscenely sharp. I could practically see the inside of his skin, wet and fleshy and pink. His heart beating. His spleen. His trachea like cartilage in a fish's skeleton.

I smiled back at him.

"Why are you making that face?"

"What face?"

"Never mind." He looked into my eyes and then shook his head quickly as if he was disoriented. "Okay we'll get a bike. Happy?" He squinted and reached around for his shirt. It fluttered up against his chest before he put it on.

"Yeah. You'll like it. You really will Danny."

"Like what?" he smiled. "Oh, the motorcycle, yeah."

I lit two cigarettes and gave one to him. The smell of the herb shop blew past; sage, lavender, cedar, all burning somewhere in a bowl, drifting through the winding alleys and then out to us, up to heaven. The girl with the eye necklace and the gum would pour the ashes tomorrow morning and they would blow, black, gray, and white specks circling back, catching in the light as she shuts the blue door to keep in the cold.

That night I dreamed about Danny and his camping stove and when I woke up the sky was pale and I was alone on the plateau, freezing. Stars were fading. The sea made itself out to be real instead of an internal sound. It hushed against the cliffsides. I lay on my back, smoking until it was light, and the morning sickness had passed.

Then I wondered what year it was. It was always hard to remember. How old was I? It seemed like I had been answering the word "eighteen" to that question for years. I knew that before this I lived somewhere else by myself, and before that with my brother, and before that with my parents. And before that I wasn't alive. But it was all as if I wasn't alive. It was all as if I had just crawled out of the Aegean, wet and hungry.

I thought I might be nineteen already. I thought of Odysseus' bed, carved from a tree, growing up through the floor of his house. I thought of sun-burnt yellow land that stretched in endless plains over dry dirt. I thought of a field of sunflowers I had seen from a train in Yugoslavia, that was as vast as a field of wheat I had seen from a car in America. I thought of my muscles, my Achilles tendon, rubbed raw into a thick callused chord. I thought of myself buried and exhumed. Waiting in the dirt, in a block of cement to be reincarnated.

"When I've seen enough," I said out loud to see how it'd sounded when I'd said it to my brother.

Then I thought of a song and sang it quietly and loudly, getting to the end and starting over. I had not heard myself sing since elementary school. My voice was nothing. It was barely audible to me no matter how loud I tried to sing.

And though I walk home alone
I might walk home alone
But my faith in love is still devout.

I pulled out a cigarette and rummaged through Danny's pack for a flannel shirt to put on. I tried to sing every song I could remember. Tried to picture heaven. Heaven was inside the body of an animal. Or in the ocean. Dark, warm, weightless, painless, like being drunk. Like never having to sober up, never having to speak.

I reached in my pocket for a pack of matches and found the paper from Stephan. A big half circle was torn out of it. I opened it up. It was in English, an advertisement for ground beef that Stephan must have believed had some magical properties. I laughed. Probably testing a theory that he could taste the food in the picture. Probably could. I lit my cigarette and turned the paper over, squinted at it.

...the season safe and relaxing. But there are other tales of tourists losing more than just their possessions. Violent crime is another unpleasant reality to keep in mind while touring abroad, as we have seen most recently in the tragic death of nineteen-year-old Jeremy Lethe. Lethe's parents brought their son

home from holiday in Greece, thinking that he had an advanced case of hepatitis. Less than one day later Lethe died in an Essex hospital. Though Lethe did have liver damage, an autopsy determined the actual cause of death to be a ruptured spleen, apparently caused by blunt trauma. Lethe's parents are still looking for any inf...

I stopped reading and threw the paper quickly over the cliffside and wiped my hands on the front of my shirt. It blew away, rose up over the dark purple water and I pushed the collar of my shirt up over my lips to catch the blood as it ran down.

21

Air rushed over our bodies and we could taste salt and fine powdery dirt, feel it sticky on our skin and in our hair. Danny held me around the waist clasping his hands around his elbows. The roads were narrow and covered with pebbles and stones.

I fought against the urge to close my eyes and lost. I closed them for five seconds, then seven, then nine, fifteen, thirty. My ribs ached with suppressed hysteria. The island was small and full of hills and black volcanic rock and miles of deserted coastline. We were headed west for a place called Golden Beach but I didn't want to get there. I wanted only to stay on these empty shore roads, going fast.

It was bright and hot. And I felt like we were finally going as fast as we should have been in the first place. The road rose before us, bringing the coastline into perfect view, ships and boats and bespeckled beaches. Yellow grass, lone olive trees scattered at a distance from one another, here and there a house, a stone wall, a dune we could not see beyond.

The dirt road met up with a wider paved road that stretched back in towards the center of the island. We followed it without seeing any cars or buses until we had practically reached Golden Beach, where another small town unfolded, paved with asphalt not brick. The buildings were taller then those in the port town and the architecture more square. There was glass in the windows, not just shutters. There were colors other than blue. It was a new town. A heavily touristed town.

Blond haired people lounged and strolled. There were volleyball nets set up by the water, and an umbrella rental. I didn't think anyone slept on this beach.

We pulled in near a three story building with an enclosed terrace and big picture windows. We parked the bike near a grove of cedars, unstrapped my bag and headed down a paved road in the direction of the beach which was bordered by a low stone wall. We could see people wind surfing out in the blue, and boats anchored in the distance.

We dropped my book bag and took off our shirts and shoes.

"Can you actually swim?" I asked Danny.

"Of course."

"Can you swim as good as me? I doubt it."

He looked at me. He looked right at my breasts. I stepped closer to him, until my chest was almost touching his and flexed my bicep "I doubt it," I said again, and this time it sounded meaner than I had intended. I laughed to try to lighten it. I needed to be alone and somehow I was saddled with this poor fucker, under the auspices that we were 'traveling together,' that we were both American. But the country he was from bore little resemblance to the country I grew up in. I just wanted to get away. All of it might have been fine before I read Stephan's article. But it now wasn't.

He put his hand around my muscle. "You're very pretty, killer," he said.

We ran into the waves and got the dust off our bodies. We swam for a long time until the thirst was too great and we felt burnt. Until we were tired and cold from the water. Until I was too tired to be angry that he was alive.

*

Jezz pulled his arm back through the plate glass all at once, tearing it from the inside of the elbow almost to the wrist. That same arm, too. There would be no more piano playing.

Fucking hell, said Jack, trying to get behind him to support him as he fell back, staggered to one side, and collapsed, bleeding on the tile of the lobby.

Well, that's it, mumbled Nigel, lighting his cigarette. But I was already running down the block towards Athens Inn, in bare feet, swerving past cars at intersections. Half way there I realized I could have used the phone in the lobby to call an ambulance, that Jack was probably doing that now. But I couldn't stop. Couldn't wait. I kept running. I just kept running.

The meat of his arm would stay where it was behind my eyes and never go away. I saw his veins and I saw his bone and it was an intimacy I had long hoped for. It was real. My wraith, my doppelganger, my genius, my spectre. The object of my desire was real.

They sent him home to Olympos with stitches and codeine. And said three weeks without a drink was the right thing. But we bought him a bottle of retsina. We piled into one of the beds and read. And drank.

David came up and brought him some vitamins. Out in the hall he said to me, *no more.* Said, *he's not for you.* But he was wrong. Even dead he's still for me.

22

The building that we had passed turned out to be a hotel. Inside it was white and clean. The windows overlooked the beach and there was a small cafe where tourists sat reading and drinking in their Birkenstocks and khaki shorts.

We sat down at a table and shoved our bag and shoes beneath it.

"Amstel?"

"Yes, please."

Danny walked to the counter and bought our beers. It was cool inside and bright, and the tables were small.

The second I touched the cold bottle there was a change in my body, a release. I felt it in my spine. I could smell the beer. I loved the shape of the bottle, how it was wet, and the paper label was wet with beads of condensation. I breathed deeply, relaxed, pleased, watched the pale gray fog rise from the neck of the bottle and begin to drift across the mouth. I curled the dark bottle perfectly in my hand and brought it's mouth to mine, tucked my top lip neatly beneath it's top lip and brought my tongue to its bottom where it fit perfectly, as it always had, on the cold glass. I supported it on my bottom lip, letting my tongue slip into the mouth so that its underside could make contact with the smooth curved inside, just for a second. I tilted it gently, and let the beer fill my mouth and throat. I drank. I drank it all at once in long gulps. I felt lighter. My shoulders and arms broke out in goose bumps. My lips were wet with drink and saliva. My belly was full, and full of joy. I laughed as I put the bottle down. I reached across the table for the cigarettes and lit one, sitting back, and I smoked.

Danny was still drinking his beer. He lit a cigarette off mine and looked through the pack for more drachmas. His black hair now had hundreds of red strands running through it, and freckles had come out on his face. His hair was damp and stuck straight up. He handed me a few bills across the table.

I went and got more beer for us. The cafe was beautiful. It was quiet. Full of sunlight and dread and melancholy. It was full of dust motes and people who couldn't seem to see each other. Like home was, years before John came to get me. Pieces of a tea cup are imbedded in the wall from the force of being thrown so hard. But it looks almost like art. There are bugs in the cupboard crawling through the flour and sugar and pancake mix, they have veined, translucent, papery wings. Invisible. Closed up. A whole community at work. The needle on the record player is caught between the label and the last song. It makes two barely audible clicks like a tiny heart beat over and over and over, soothing. And you're lying on the white livingroom rug that's grainy and sticky and smells like dog piss, playing with a mummified seahorse that floats in water in a plastic box. A present from some friend of your mothers. You rattle it and hold it upside down. At first you think it's alive and that's just the way seahorses are. And then you think it's plastic made from a mold. And then you know it's dead, and the white eye sockets are empty. Eventually someone comes into the room and says 'shut up' and you realize for the first time that you've been singing. And you're glad they're there. Grateful like when you see the city of Athens for the first time. Grateful like when you wake up drunk at dusk.

I brought the beers back to the table. Danny was watching some British kids I hadn't noticed before. They seemed serious about their drinks. They seemed to be dressed in their only clothes. They were out of place. Not loud, but they had pulled three tables together to sit as a group. A cloud of smoke hung above them, cards and bottles covered the table.

I sat back and drank my beer.

"Are you gonna stop humming that song at some point?" Danny asked.

"Hmm?"

He smiled. He lay his hand on the middle of table, palm up. I looked at it briefly. He wanted me to lay my hand on top of his. And I would, I really would I thought, when I was done thinking.

The table of British boys raised their voices in unison to greet someone and I looked over. That's when my blood started flowing in the opposite direction. Things got lighter and I started to sweat.

"He's probably real," I said.

"What?"

I drank my entire beer and then looked again at them again out of the corners of my eyes. They were a little louder now. Then quiet all at once. Someone was telling a joke and you could hear them, silent, focused on the storyteller's melodic accent.

"He's real, I think." But maybe not, I thought, maybe he's the same as Jezz.

"Who's real? That black kid?" Danny picked his hand off the table and ran it through his hair exhaling loudly and squinting distractedly at the other table.

I bent down to put on my boots, then sat back up to see if he was still there. Punchline. Laughter. Bottles clinking. Back to quiet conversation. I stood up and walked to the middle of the room to get a better look at Jack. He was tipping back in his chair. Smiling. Wearing new clothes. He set his beer on the table. And then he spotted me.

"Hey!" He jumped up from his chair. He beamed. Started laughing immediately. "Ar'ray it's little Maya!" He grabbed me and crushed me in his arms. "Alright, our kid," he laughed.

I buried my face in his chest and held on to him. I squeezed him hard and looked up at his face, his wide jaw, perfect teeth and smashed up nose. His hair was short, sticking up in tiny yellowed dreads. I could feel his ribs.

"Jesus Christ, Jack! What are you—?"

"I'm livin here. I found a house sit, like."

"Nobody knew where you were." I laughed and let go of him. "You look great, man. You really do. I mean, what's with the clothes? You look.... God! A house sit huh?" I hugged him again and he picked me up and held me like I was a little kid with my arms around his neck. He walked back over to his table.

"This is Maya Brennan!" he said. "She's me boyfriend's wife."

They all laughed and he winked at me.

Danny stood up and brought his beer over to the table .

"Danny. Jack. Jack. Danny."

Jack shifted me on to his hip and shook Danny's hand. "Pull up a chair, luv," he said, grinning. And Danny did.

Jack sat down and held me on his lap and drank his beer. Danny sat at the table introducing himself, chatting. Waiting to get dealt into their game.

"How's a Holy Land? Hot, eh?" He bounced me on his knee.

"Fine."

"I'm thinking of goin' if I ever get another passport issued. I still haven't gone to the consulate? Bloody Jezz, you know? 'Ah...sorry, I'll ged it back faw yuh, I prohmise,'" he said, in a slurred London accent and laughed. "Jesus...I'll end up like Whipple Perry."

"Or Jens Christensen," I said.

He ignored it. We looked at each other. His face an utter stranger's, but so perfectly clear and unchanged.

"You look good, fairy. Stronger. You've really gained some weight, yeah?" His eyes moved over my face and then down to my stomach. He looked up into my eyes again and a faint puzzled smile played across his lips. He had flickers of expressions, and mannerisms that belonged to Jezz, and they passed over him like long shadows cast across a landscape, by clouds or things unseen.

"I thought you were a ghost when I saw you just now," I told him.

He shook his head. "That is not the case."

"Who's round?" I asked the table.

Someone went up for more Amstel and Danny got another chair. I slid into his.

"How's Athens?" Jack asked. "Who's there now?" he asked trying to sound disinterested. "Jezz there?"

I shook my head. "David, Stephan, Nigel, Mike. Allen and Lewis."

He laughed. "And Jezz?"

"Jezz died."

His face fell and he closed his eyes. He breathed out a kind of disgusted laugh through his nose. "Where?"

"Olympos," I said taking a beer from Danny as he passed a few around the crowded tables.

"When?" he was still shaking his head.

"A few weeks ago, I guess."

That hurt him like it had me. "Of what?"

"Natural causes." We scoffed in unison.

We touched our bottles and spilled a drop to the floor then drank. His eyes welled up and he looked past me.

"Someone called his parents to come and get him." I laughed without knowing I would and then stopped. I felt relieved just talking to him.

"Get his body?"

"I guess."

He drank his beer. "He missed you, yeah?"

"Is that what he said?"

"No of course not. He talked about you, though."

"Oh. I never talked about him."

"No," Jack said sarcastically. "Who would?" We drank like we used to but Jezz did not show up. The group played cards while Jack and I talked, and forgot what it was we were talking about. It was still bright out, but it seemed late, some limit had been reached. The sense of heat outside, the intoxication, and the waning afternoon brought on weariness.

But still we sat for a long time with nothing to say in that beautiful room. We'd have said something if either of us knew more, but we didn't. Right? We didn't. We had found each other and that was what mattered. And we could look into each other's eyes again, eyes that had shone with the same pleasures and eyes that now shone with the same unspoken warning, tell me, don't tell me. Eyes that implied words that never left our throats.

"How 'bout you and your mate come back to me house and eat n'shower, like," Jack said. He started to get up but then changed his mind and sat back down, heavily. Looked over at me shook his head, and laughed. We were both drunk. "'To stand now is no small feat, he said soulfully.'"

I stood up unsteadily and held his head against my stomach, and he wrapped his drunken arms around me. His shirt was so blue and clean. I could smell it. He smelled like clean sheets. He smelled like balsam soap. I wanted to stay close to him, hold him. Hold his hands. I wanted to cry. So I stood there for several minutes trying to cry. But I forgot what I was doing, and just ended up staring out the window behind him. Breathing. Smelling his clothes and the beer on his breath and breathing.

23

The house was a low bungalow style building, partially built into the cliffside, with sliding glass doors and a deck that ran around the side which faced the sea. He led us up the wide white concrete steps to the front door and unlocked it, stepping inside and setting his keys on the top of a bookcase. He had taken good care of the place. If he had thrown any parties it wasn't evident. I hadn't been in a house for several years, and it was very nice. It was not as I had expected.

The cold tile floors were covered with blue rugs. Bookshelves lined the walls. Paintings, obviously done by a friend or member of the family hung throughout a long hall. The living room was filled with tiny knickknacks and mismatched furniture. He walked directly to the couch which was piled with books and started shuffling through them. There were three separate piles, one looked like children's books in Greek. There was a notebook lying on the floor half tucked under the couch.

"Look, My," he said, "I've managed to get a hold of these." He held up John Donne's Holy Sonnets. It was a hardback and the spine was weak. "But I've got to teach meself Greek," he said. "Because I've no opportunities, like, for buying books in English. This one was a lucky find, y'don't even know. C'med, see the rest uh the house."

He walked along in front of us still holding his book of poems. A long hallway lead to a large tiled kitchen, which lead to the deck. The hallway opened into three bedrooms, and a bathroom.

We went out to the deck and spit over the side into the sea. Jack stood behind us holding his open book in one hand and flipping the pages with the other.

"This is more like it," said Danny.

We paced around the deck looking out at the landscape and water, and Jack went in to get beer. Then we sat on the rail and drank some more.

"Where are the people who live here?" I asked.

"In America, like."

"Doing what?"

"The woman who owns the house is some kind of teacher or somethin. She's usually here all summer, like, but not this summer. She took her husband and kid to the States. I guess the kid never got to go before. I want to work out a thing like, where I can do this whenever they're gone."

"Lucky," I said.

"That's me middle name," he said. "C'med, come in and see the rooms and bath, like." He lead us around with drunken grace, with that cautious hospitality you have for certain friends and strangers.

Danny and I separated our few possessions and tossed them into separate rooms.

"I'm sleeping in here off the deck," said Jack. "There's soap and all sorts of lovely shit in the shower."

I went into a bedroom and looked around. It belonged to a child. The sheets were pale blue, printed with pictures of tiny high heeled shoes, little black dogs, and little bows. I opened the window and a wave of warm air entered the cool room. I shut it again. There were framed pictures on the walls. A horse. A beach at sunset—Golden Beach probably. And the Virgin Mary.

I tossed my stuff on the floor and lay on the bed. The springs were shot and squeaky and I could feel them. Danny came and stood in the doorway smiling.

"I told you Jack was lucky," I told him.

"And you were right," he said condescendingly, for no good reason.

Jack looked in over Danny's shoulder, "I'm goin to market. Squid and what else?"

I reached in my pocket for some money and handed him a thousand drachmas. "Lots of food. No ouzo, okay?"

"Ta'ra Americans," he called as he walked out the door. We heard him starting the motorcycle. Danny looked anxiously at me and I got up and went down the hall to the bathroom.

There was a wall-sized mirror, a sink, tub and shower with a glass door. There were even towels. I sat on the toilet and took my boots off. They were worn and full of sand I tossed them in a corner. Took off my clothes and put them in the sink. Then I was naked looking in the mirror. I was very tan except for the line left by my shorts. My body was lean. I could see my ribs and the bone sticking up between them. And I could see just how round my stomach was, just how much my breasts had grown. It wasn't right. The body was no longer just mine, but some softer, malformation of a pubescent body; the breasts and rounded belly coupled with a shaved head and wide jaw. And a look that just didn't belong. The body was changing like some unexpected horror from a science fiction film. My breasts were sore. I pressed my hands over them. I still had my biceps. I flexed in the mirror. I smiled at myself. My teeth were filthy and yellow so I stopped smiling.

I turned on the shower and let it run while I rubbed a soapy finger over my teeth, and then I got in. Dirt and sand ran into the drain. I felt the salt washing away. I rubbed a big green balsam smelling bar of soap all over myself. I sat and scrubbed my feet and hairy legs. My skin was breathing again. I scrubbed my head and then stood there letting the water burn me until it was no longer hot. And then I stood there until it was too cold and my heart was pounding and I was awake. "Clean," my body thought, turning off the tap.

I dried off and ran my hands over my head, drops of water sprang up from the short straight hairs. I looked, from the neck up, as I always had, like a little boy. I wrapped up in a big gray towel, grabbed my clothes and walked out.

Music was playing in the house. Loud Greek music. Danny was going through the kitchen cupboards, peering at cookbooks that he couldn't read and drinking another beer.

I walked out on to the deck and shook out my sandy clothes, then went back in the house and washed them in the bathroom sink with the green soap. The water turned black. I rinsed them and let them soak.

When I went back in to talk to Danny he was drinking what looked to be his fourth pint, his feet slapping the cold tile to the off beat of the music. He was smiling, quietly looking down with the beer held close to his body, the veins in his bare and hairless arms defined, his shoes off. There was nothing to say to him.

I squeezed out my shirt and shorts and hung them on the deck. My hair was already dry. I ran my fingers through it feeling no dirt or sand in my scalp then I took the towel off spread it on the deck and lay on my stomach. I watched the water below move like a massive fire, too heavy to rise up. It rushed and shattered, scattering droplets like little sparks, perfect tiny spheres that arced. Worlds that spun.

24

A pair of bare feet came suddenly into focus, and a shadow fell across my face.

"You're naked."

I looked up at him. "Yeah."

"There's food and more Amstel and I bought more fags." He grabbed my shirt off the rail and tossed it at me. "Jesus. Look at you. C'med, you can borrow some of me shorts," he said.

I snapped him with the shirt. "Man, I am really starving."

"Even me," he said. "Now put your fuckin kit on. And come eat some food."

We cut open the little squids and took out their hollow plastic insides. We dipped them in flour and salt and fried them. We piled them on brown and white paper bags on the counter. Then we piled them on our plates and squeezed lemon over them, shoving their little rubbery bodies into our mouths. We drank retsina and more retsina, putting our plates to the side with a pile of lemon rinds and wedges.

We lay on the deck and watched the sun fall below the sea. When night came up all around us and down upon us we were happy. We were so happy in the dark. Jack lit candles and set them around the deck to keep the mosquitoes away. We lay lazily trying to force the last of the calamari down. I had distended my stomach. Without beer I was in danger of death.

"Beer," I said.

"Shut up," Danny said, lying on his back with his arms spread wide. He had been in a strange mood since we left the cafe and I couldn't really cheer him up.

"I'm serious," I said.

The stars had come out.

"And I'm fucking serious," Danny said. "Shut up."

"Faggot," I said smiling at him. I thought that was funny.

"I'll show you who's a faggot," he said.

"Motherfucker," I said. I wanted to be joking, but realized the second I started to speak that I wasn't. I got up to walk inside. I could feel his desire for himself as it reflected off my skin. He couldn't know that these things only go one way. That I had already left the mind and my all consuming project now was how to leave the body.

He grabbed my leg, pulling it across his chest with greater force than I could have anticipated, knocking me off balance so that I landed on my back with my legs on his chest. I brought my knees up and hit him with both of my feet in the side, hard, hard enough to push myself across the deck on my back. I rolled over quickly and started to push myself back up. He grabbed my ankles and pulled me back toward him. I twisted and sat up but he lifted my legs straight, pushed my ankles over my head and crawled over me so that the back of my legs rested on his shoulders, then he lay on me with all his weight, pressing my thighs to my chest. He smiled at me and moved his face close very close to mine, breathing heavily from the exertion. His hair fell in front of his face. I looked at his beautiful straight teeth and the curve of his neck.

I smiled at him and then punched him hard in the face. His head jerked back. His nose began to bleed on me, into my eyes and mouth. I turned my head, couldn't breathe. He grabbed my wrists and pushed my arms down hard against the deck. I was starting to feel cold. My hands were wet and sticky and one of them was falling asleep. It was ridiculous. I started to laugh. I laughed so hard I started to hyperventilate.

Finally Danny got up. He held out his hand to me. I raised my arm and he grabbed my wrist and pulled me to my feet. Like it was the end of a circus trick. Ta dah! I stood in front of him breathing hard, and looked at him. His face was covered with blood and saliva and he looked shocked, like he wasn't used to this. Like he wasn't happy.

Jack was looking up at the sky. It sounded like he was talking to someone else. I looked over to see who it was, but just caught a glimpse of his back as he went inside.

"You okay?" Danny asked.

"Yeah."

"Good," he said. Then he punched me in the eye, knocking me to the deck. He pulled me to my feet by my shirt and punched me again in the same eye. I fell back a few steps. It felt like this time he had broken my cheekbone. My face was hot. My vision was blurry and two dimensional. I heard air rushing inside my head. I wished he hadn't done it. Then I started to laugh again.

Danny stood staring at me, wiping his nose with the back of his hand and holding a deep breath. I could see the muscles in his stomach tighten. Then it broke over us, high pitched, a painful sound in his throat. And he lay down on the deck and wept. Because there's less than nothing in being the one who delivers the blow. It's all in the receiving. There is nothing real in the delivery of blows. It changes nothing. Makes nothing happen. It was funny if you thought about it long enough. He was getting that now. His shoulders shook and he covered his face. I didn't want to fight. I was worried he would be sick; crying can make you sick, especially if you have been drinking.

"I can take a punch," I tried to reassure him. "I can take a punch, Danny, honest." Blood was running into my mouth from some place inside my head. I spit it on to the deck. I felt like my brain had bounced off the inside of my skull and my vision was starting to narrow. He was still crying, and he wouldn't even get up. He wouldn't look at me. Now's the time when you're supposed to say okay—let's just go play cards or something, let's go play dominoes, or build a model, but he wouldn't even do that. "Quit acting like a baby," I told him. "Jesus you little fucking boy, just suck it up." Then I thought maybe I should get him a smoke, maybe he really was upset. "Danny," I said, extending my hand to him. "Danny. Get up okay?" I tapped him a few times in the side of the head, trying to rouse him to his feet. His nose was pouring blood all over the deck. The pain in my face had dulled to a slow burning throb. And It wasn't funny anymore. I tapped him again. He put his arm up to block but I caught him in the head once more.

Finally he stood up. Tore at his hair. He walked in a circle with his hands outstretched and tense. I could see the veins in his fore arms and he was still crying. He was still crying when he knocked me out.

*

Jezz was lying next to me, one arm across my waist. His hair was longer in the front and his skin was yellow and sweaty. When he saw that my eyes were open, he pulled himself up on his elbow and rested his head on his narrow brittle hand. He smiled. He must have smelled the blood or smelled the liquor on my breath.

We meet here, he smiled gently. *I've spent a lot of time here. This is the membrane that keeps us separate. You bleed and I'll drink. I'll drink and tell you secrets.*

Did you know Jack was here?

No.

Does he know you're here?

He shrugged. *Dunno. But you do and we're together and now we can... now we can.... Watch me now.* He held a coin between his thumb and forefinger, raised his eyebrows and pushed it sideways into his skull. It disappeared. Then he grinned, leaned forward and kissed me. His mouth was cold, and so was his face, despite the sweat. But it was a lovely kiss. His lips tasted like dried mud. I pulled the coin out of my mouth and handed it back to him.

Great eh? I made a coin appear in your mouth.

You pushed it into my mouth.

Okay, he said. *Watch this. This I really did make appear.* He put his thumb on my chin and pulled my mouth open gently then reached into my mouth. He fit his entire hand in my mouth and then pushed it down my throat. I felt the pressure of his fingers moving as he tried to find something. He reached further down, his elbow rested just behind my top teeth. He gazed up as he did this, trying to concentrate on what he was looking for. I felt him pressing organs to the side.

Finally he pulled out a tiny paper cup with a goldfish in it. The fish swam around and around. We set it between us on the bed, and looked down at it. The water was shiny, and silver looking where it interfaced with the sides of the cup. The little fish was beautiful. It was oblivious to us, to everything. Completely silent. Its scales were minute arcs and half circles covering its body, protecting it, making it easier for it to slip through the water. It was shaped like an eye, but with beautifully translucent tissue on its back and tail, that glided as it guided it through the water.

Look at its fins, I told him. *You can see through them.*

You can almost see through its body, Jezz said. He smiled.

He picked up the paper cup and put it to his lips for a joke. I tried to smile again. This was a great magic trick, and he was playing it well. He dipped his boney finger into the water just above the fish and dabbed water on my forehead. He held his finger over my lips and let a drop of water fall into my mouth. It was so cold it was hot.

It made me tired. It cheered me. I felt good. I had never seen anything more alive than this fish that lived inside of me. He played with it a little while more while I dozed. They were from the same place, Jezz and this fish. Finally he set the cup back on the bed. *I can't believe it's still alive,* he said. *Do you want me to put it back or should I drink it for real?*

Put it back, I whispered. I was almost asleep. *There's beer in the fridge if you're thirsty.*

*

"My. Maya. Maya wake up." Jack was holding me on the kitchen floor with a bag of ice on my face. His voice was clear and low. My clothes felt wet and my head throbbed. My mouth was dry. It was dark. Jack leaned over my face and touched it. "She's okay," he said.

In the morning I was still on the kitchen floor. Two of my fingers were taped to strips of cardboard with electrical tape. My face had been washed but my clothes were covered with dried blood. I could see out of one eye but the other side of my face was too swollen and another eye was buried somewhere in there. My teeth hurt. I yawned and my jaw hurt, my head pounded. I got up and put water on the stove to boil, I was nauseous. When Danny came into the kitchen he started to cry again. He looked desperately sad. His face was full of bruises and his nose was swollen. He tried to sit and put his arms around me, but he was taking up the air I needed to keep from being sick.

"Quit it," I said.

He stepped back and looked at me.

"Jesus Christ," I said.

He went into the bathroom and continued crying. When the water boiled I made tea with dried mint leaves, and tried to eat some crackers to keep myself from throwing up. Then I went in to sleep on the sheets that were printed with dogs and shoes. I lay naked in the child's bed, pissed that my face was all messed up and that I had nothing to read. I put my hands on my face and felt the tight puffy skin. One side seemed pretty normal. I was happy not to have my nose broken again. I'd had my nose broken when I was eight, and I hadn't liked it. I had especially hated lying in bed looking at the decor of the room. Looking at the stuffed animals, mute, with their vacant expressions. And I remember being particularly enraged by the cover of a Highlights magazine that lay on the floor. It depicted boys and girls playing marbles and the girls wore braids. I had to cover it with a pillowcase. The combination of fucked up face, and kid's room was just bad. I didn't like it when I was a child and I liked it even less now. Just as it was then, the objects in the room seemed to have been chosen and placed for maximum irony. But then any little girl's room will do for that sort of thing, regardless of the culture.

*

"You look all right," he said. "It's nothing you can't take."

"I've already taken it."

He nodded. "Exactly."

"Where were you?" I asked him.

Jack shook his head. "I thought he was your boyfriend, like."

It looked as if saying that made him sick. "Jesus, fucking...sorry. I really just thought you could stop if you needed to. It's not like you or me never watched a fight, like. Did you never see worse happen? You just weren't fighting back. I've never seen you do that. Y'fuckin offered him a fag in the middle of it. What am I supposed to think?" He was talking fast. He stood by me and rubbed his hand over my scalp, looked at my face. He looked into my eye like you look for complicity, a complicity of love or sex or silence. He stood patiently beside me with his eyes in mine until he found it. And finding it, knowing it himself so well, he smiled in recognition. We looked at one another like you look at the city after visiting the Parthenon. Once we were part of a greater thing, but it could barely be imagined.

25

Danny lay on his stomach reading the paper with his shirt wrapped around his head. Some kind of ointment he had put on was melting in the heat and shone greasily on his nose and cheek. He was very tanned now, and needed a haircut. He looked like he was really touring now. The restless tour. He had been cauterized by the sun, and it became him. He was beautiful to me now. Bruised and tan and drunk.

He opened another Amstel with his teeth. "Hey, My, I'm gonna cut out of here today." He flipped on to his back and lay with his hands behind his head. "I want to get to Turkey before I end up staying another whole day in Athens. Or something. I got to get moving. I feel like a fucking asshole sitting around doing nothing. Do you want to come?"

"Nah." We looked at one another's faces. His nose was still swollen.

He wrote out his parents' address for me. "Maybe we can see each other back in the States," he said.

I shook his hand and then hugged him. He took a breath and his arms encircled me. He really was lonely in a way I couldn't understand. I saw him in that moment and liked him, like that first day on the train platform.

"Sorry about your eye," he said.

26

"Alone at last," Jack said. "Don't think we've ever been, eh? There's always been a body between us, like." He rinsed out empty beer bottles and put them to the side of the sink while he talked. Then he filled the tea kettle and set it on the burner. The blue flames reflected against its silver bottom. "You'd like some tea, fairy?"

"Yes, please."

"You're face is quite fucked up, like. Your fairy face. I know what its like, yeah?"

I nodded.

He got some honey and bread out of the cupboard and set them on the table. He handed me a spoon. He moved quickly, coordinated like soldiers were, possessed by an unconscious grace. There was a competence in each of his gestures. He put two mugs filled with mint leaves on the table and poured boiling water over them, then he covered them with little yellow saucers and sat down across from me. He was wearing his swim trunks and his hair stuck up in an unruly mass of tiny discolored knots. He leaned back and crossed his legs beneath the table. And then composed himself as if he were about to make a speech. He cleared his throat.

"I am a li'l world made cunningly," he said. "Of elements and an angelic sprite. Do you know that one?" he asked excitedly.

"Isn't cunningly another word for oral sex?" I asked.

"C'med, My. Do you know it or not?"

I nodded, chewing a piece of bread. I took a quick sip of tea. "But black sin hath betrayed to endless night my world's both parts," I said. I raised my eyebrows, and winked with the eye that worked. "And O both parts must die."

He smiled broadly and leaned back stretching, spreading his arms wide. "Ah, yeah. I'm so glad you're here."

"Shall I set it to the U.S. national anthem?" I asked. "Want me to sing it?"

He laughed. "You'd make our boy proud but Nah. Say it. Say the whole thing, like." He stood now and came round to my chair. He knelt and lay his head in my lap.

"I don't know it all," I lied. "It's about a fire."

He pressed the top of his head gently against my stomach. "Pour new seas in mine eyes so that I might drown my world with my weeping earnestly, or wash it if it must be drowned no more. Now say the rest," he said. I looked down at his broad back, and rested my hands there.

"But O, it must be burnt, alas the fire of lust and envy have burnt it heretofore. Let their flames retire, and burn me O lord with a fiery zeal." And then I did sing the last part like the national anthem "O-of thee and thy-yy house, which doth in e-ea-ting heal."

He laughed and stood abruptly, pulling me up. "C'med now."

He lead me down the hall and into his room. There were books on the floor. On the table beside his bed stood half a bottle of ouzo, an ashtray and a flashlight. There was a picture of Jack and Jezz taken in a photo-booth taped to the cover of a book of poetry. In it they smiled and their cheeks touched. They looked like kids. Jack already looked strangely older now than he did in the picture. He sat down on the bed and began leafing through a volume John Donne.

"I'm not done with Donne," he said. He uncapped the ouzo and took a drink, holding it out to me. I shook my head and he put it down, still looking at the page. I sat cross legged on the floor and averted my eyes from the photograph. Jack didn't speak. It seemed he just wanted company while he read. We were silent for some time. But our quiet bodies passed information from one to another. Had some long nostalgic conversation, comforted one another it seemed, with their very existence.

"I don't have any pictures of him," I said finally.

"No, you've somethin better, like, don't you?"

"What's that?"

He looked up from the book straight at me. "How do you get by pretending, my little fairy?" Then he knelt beside me and kissed me on my bruised cheek. "You pretend with me, even now that we're alone, yeah? You'll pretend you can't hear me anymore if I say the wrong thing, like. If I say stay, you'll leave. If I say leave, you'll stay." He kissed me on the mouth. "It was something like that right? You remember, yeah? Do you remember how to kiss?"

I nodded and put my arms around him and he sat on the floor and pulled me into his lap, touching my neck, running his palm over my short hair, over my scalp. He pulled my shirt up over my head, holding it out so it wouldn't touch my swollen eye.

"We've done this before, yeah?"

"Yeah."

He ran his hand over my breasts then leaned down to put his mouth on my collarbone. The picture of he and Jezz lay on the book beside us smiling up into empty space. I watched Jack glance down at it. I watched him close his eyes. I kissed the back of his neck and slid closer to him to wrap my legs around his waist. To rest my hands on his shoulders. To better feel his restlessness beneath me. I leaned forward and pressed him down and lay my head against his neck.

He slid his swim shorts off and lay naked on the tile. Our chests pressed together. His legs touching mine, intertwined, curve to curve and tendon to tendon. My hand rested in his wide knuckled hand.

"You're pregnant," he said.

"Yeah."

He smiled and put his lips against mine. "So stop lying now," he whispered into my mouth. He ran his hands down my back and tucked them into my shorts, slid them over my hips. He pushed them down to my scarred ankles and I shook them off. I sat up straddling him and he ran his hands over the small curve of my belly. My woman's body above his fighter's defined form. My muscles lean and tired, my skin growing taut around what was left of my boy life, my runner's life, the last map of our lover's life.

"I'm pregnant," I said.

He laughed, his eyelids were heavy. "Yeah," he said, and held me by the hips, eased me down against him. Held my thighs. Then he pulled me forward by the shoulders wrapped me up in his arms, tight against his chest, one hand cupped over the back of my head. He kissed my cheek from time to time as we lay there, as we moved there slowly, and he spoke in a quiet voice. His breath smelled like licorice and cigarettes. Light narrowed and dimmed in the room. And he began to cry.

27

"Holy fuck, My. I think I killed him. I think I killed him, fairy."

"What do you mean?" I whispered. "Did you get in a fight?"

"No."

I exhaled. I couldn't speak out loud. "Did you. What did you do?" I stood up and opened the curtains to let light fill the room. I opened the windows wide and felt the warm salt air come in. The tile was cold on my bare feet. And my body felt good, like after a long run. I didn't want him to cry. "What?" I whispered again.

"I thought I was helpin im, like." He looked at my face, and he didn't look pained, but relieved. He got up and opened the closet and pulled out his pack. He turned it upside down on the bed and eight or nine passports fell out.

"These were.... Are these new?"

He nodded. "He was a fuck-wit. He was not sober even for an hour at a time, like. Y've no idea, yeah? I thought if he held on to these he'd be fucked for sure. I wanted him to come with me. But he said y'd be back and then y'wouldn't be able t'find us. Jokes on him right? Y'found me, alright yeah? Somehow. My wife, he'd say, My wife is coming back. Do you know, yeah? how many times we had to hear the word wife?"

"Why do you have these?" I whispered.

"D'y think it was good, like, what happened in the airport? Do you think it was worth a thousand quid?" He sat naked on the edge of the bed. "I don't. I took them so he wouldn't get in trouble. But I think, My. I think he'd already made the sale, yeah? And I was already gone, with these. And I think somebody took their fee out of him, like, when he couldn't deliver," he looked up and his voice sounded hoarse. "Its me. The more I think about it. Its me what screwed him. And now these," he said picking up a passport and dropping it. "It's eight thousand pounds. And you need it. You'd be set with it."

I shook my head. "I did read about a kid from Essex with Jezz's name, getting beat up in Greece," I told him. Jezz had started his flirtation with dying long before either of us had left, and we both knew the jealousy of it. "But It doesn't mean anything. It doesn't mean you're right."

"You left, then I left, and he was all alone with David."

"Which means he was safe," I said. "He always got hurt. He got hurt when we were around there was nothing we could do. You're not right. It's not you."

Tears slid down his face and spilled onto his chest. I could hear every sentence that I had ignored and the ones that weren't even said yet. The world seemed incredibly simple in that moment. I wiped his eyes with the heel of my palm. I sat next to him on the bed and looked at the passports, set them aside one by one. Twenty-thousand dollars worth. How handy would that be now? I wouldn't use it to buy drinks. The difference between want and need was making itself clear once again. I lay my head in Jack's lap and looked up at him.

"Leaving a person doesn't count for killing them," I said.

*

John opened Screwy's mouth and gently pulled on the long tongue. It hung out of the dogs tiny head, looked ridiculous. We stood back by the garage next to a small hole we had dug. John held the tongue out straight from the dog's head and gripped the tip of it in his teeth. He growled and shook his head from side to side so it looked like he and Screwy were fighting for the tongue.

Quit it, I told him.

He's dead, John said through clenched teeth. *There's nothing in there anymore.*

C'mon, I said. *Cut it out.*

Oh, Jesus Christ, he said. *It's not hurting him. He's dead.* And he bit off the tip of screwy's tongue and spit it into his hand *See?* His lips were covered with the dog's blood. He smiled and the lines in between his teeth were red. *You do it.* He shook the piece of tongue off his hand and rubbed his red palm against his jeans. Then he held the tongue out to me. *C'mon, Screwy's not in there.* He opened the dog's mouth wide. It was wet and red. *Scrrreeeewwwyyyyy,* he called down the throat. *See? No answer. Come on.*

No.

It'll make you feel better.

Unh uh.

I'm telling you.

I held the dogs tongue which was flat and missing a piece. The tongue was bright with blood and it was getting on his fur.

This isn't going to make me feel any better at all, I said.

Watch, he said. *I'll do it again.* And he put the tongue between his teeth and let the dogs body hang while he shrugged. *Nothing to it,* he said through clenched teeth.

I hit the dog in the head with the side of the shovel and he fell from John's mouth onto the grass with a dull thud. There was dirt on John's face from the shovel and his lips were bright and shiny. He looked completely shocked, half smiling, trying to decide what to do next. I started to run as fast as I could toward the apartment but he caught up in a couple of strides and grabbed my arm, jerked me backwards on to the ground.

MOM! I screamed. I hadn't meant to. *Mom Mom Mom!* I shrieked. He had me pinned and he had some dirt and scratches on his face, and the dogs blood, and he looked shocked. But then he started laughing and rolled over on to the grass next to me. He covered his mouth and laughed hard and his eyes began to run.

Mom? he said, and laughed. *Mom Mom Mom?*

He held his stomach and tears streamed down his face. He cried hard. I rolled around next to him. I wiped my eyes. My sides hurt from laughing so hard. I though I might piss my pants.

Mom! Mom! Mom! We lay on our backs, holding hands and screaming together while Screwy and the shovel lay stiff and mute, lost somewhere in the grass. *Mom. Mom. Mom!* We called out to no one. And no one answered.

*

Jack and I woke already kissing. It was dark in the room. He smelled like ouzo, sweet and oxidizing in the air all around him. He ran his fingers over my scalp. The windows were still open and the moonlight shone in and touched every surface. My eye was crusty and swollen shut but I wasn't in pain. I curled my body into his. I had forgotten how much I loved to sleep next to him. I had loved to sleep with both of them. That drunken heavy sleep, many arms and legs crossing and the lean weight of only muscle. I loved the way we would nearly wake and turn, to be held one way or the other. Or the way we held Jezz. Our bodies were the bodies he had loved, and we loved him now in our half sleep, though he was gone, and would never wake. He would never again wake, as we had, from being kissed.

We dressed and put the passports in our pockets. We walked through the dark hall and out by the front door, we walked down a little path that lead underneath the deck. The water at low tide, lapped at a narrow strip of sand below the cliff, and we went down to this little beach in the darkness. The water was black but for where, in its movements and crests, it caught the moonlight and shimmered.

We tossed the little books out on the ground and didn't bother to look at the photographs, names, visas, nationalities. We spread the covers out flat and raised the pages in the middle and set them at the edge of the beach in a line, like a fleet. Then we lit the center pages with a match. The yellow light illuminated our task beneath the deck and threw shadow upon our surroundings. We poked the passports out into the sea one by one with a long thin stick and they drifted. Toy boats on fire. Little lanterns. They lit up the black water beneath them. The orange glow of those closer to the shore lit our faces from below and cast our eyes in shadow. We took off our clothes and went into the warm water and swam beside the little fires. We swam until each one had burned out and the water was black again. And we treaded water waiting for our eyes to adjust to the darkness. I floated on my back to look up at the expanse of stars. I drifted, while Jack swam. And I thought about where to go now. How to get there. Where to leave from. I'd have to go home to Olympos first.

I don't know where my indiscriminate faithlessness comes from. And I doubt if knowing helps. At some point you come to look at events and information as a picture. Like staring at words in a book—

not reading anymore but staring—seeing instead all the spaces—all the little spaces between the words connecting like insect trails, like mazes. Little hallways of their own. But they lead nowhere. And tell you nothing. Give you nothing. Like the crumbling and random stone walls you see sometimes in the hillsides on the way to Corinth, built by some farmer some centuries ago. And somehow they're pleasing. These relics you can't believe haven't been given a good hard kick yet—to get it over with. To just once and for all get it gone. Because these things aren't like the grass and the trees, these things aren't like us, having the decency to die and be born. These things are just a kind of muteness. An absence. A tyranny. The tyranny of the object this time, and we're supposed to worship it the longer it manages to avoid getting swept away. We're not supposed to touch it with our skin, our hands. It makes me sick. It makes me love those soldiers who shot the face off the sphinx. Why shouldn't it all die too? Why should it stay to mock us with it's degenerate inexplicable nothingness. We are the words and these things are the spaces. The blank spaces we can never keep ahead of.

I dipped below the surface and swam to the little strip of sand. Jack had his clothes back on and he was sitting with his legs drawn up, looking at the water.

Jezz sat beside him facing out to sea, his dark outline barely visible. The beads of sweat on his brow picked up the light that shone. He almost shimmered.

I stood there before them naked in the darkness and warm night air. "I see him," I told Jack.

"No," he said without looking up. "You don't."

28

"I'm leaving."

"Of course you are."

"I left gear at Olympos, and I need to pick it up. But I'll come back."

"No you won't."

"Well I hope my leaving doesn't kill you. If you drink too much and fall down the stairs, I'll be to blame for it I guess."

"I'm ignoring you, fairy." He turned the page of his Greek/English dictionary and jotted something down in a notebook.

"Well, I wish you felt better," I said. And it was true.

He shook his head. Then he stood up abruptly, came to the door and pressed me against it. He held my face and looked into my eyes "Kiss me," he said. "Kiss me like he kissed."

And I did, for a long time.

Kiss me like he kissed, I thought.

And he did.

29

David walked on to the platform carrying a yellow plastic sports bottle, the kind campers always carry. He was in good spirits and happy I was back.

"What's with the bottle?" I asked, looking up at him from the bench.

"It's a handy little thing I picked up while you were away." He flashed a toothy grin. "But look at me tiny electric fan!" He pulled out a miniature battery operated fan, the kind you can hold in your hand. It had a little plastic propeller that blows air at you, and he loved the novelty of it. He turned it on. "Put your finger in it."

"No."

He laughed, "C'mon, put your finger in it."

"Unh-uh."

"Oh all right, be a baby."

He put the fan back in the pocket of his jean jacket and sat down next to me eating his cookies.

It was early and only about ten runners were milling around the station, smoking and passing bottles. The train would be late, but I didn't care. I just wanted to sit with David, and talk. I felt right then that I had missed him, missed his presence, his mannerism, his weight.

"Look at you," he said. He held my face in his hands "I'd almost say you look healthy, but for this eye." He ran his thumb softly over my cheekbone and temple, and looked closely at me. "Did you get in a fight?"

"No."

He laughed. "So Black Jack's got a house sit, eh?"

"Yeah, until August."

"He'll be back down begging on Omonia Square by September."

"Maybe," I said. "Maybe he'll get a job somewhere. He's learning Greek."

"People who drink like that don't get real work. They can't pick and they can't wait tables. The fucking kibbutzim don't even want them. They run trains, or beg, or steal."

I nodded. "But Jack's not doing any of that."

He rolled his eyes. Smirked at me. "What did you talk about?"

"Not much. I was sick most of the time I was there."

He nodded. "You tell him about Jezz?"

"Yeah."

"What did he say?"

"He felt bad."

"What island was it?" he asked.

"Mykonos," I lied.

Some runners were sitting in a circle on the platform, drinking and folding leaflets. It wasn't such a bad job. It kept you fed, gave you a place to live. People to talk to. I looked around for Stephan and Mike but they weren't there. I even looked for Nigel. Everyone appeared vaguely familiar. No one came to sit with us. And the air felt lighter and cleaner than I had remembered it. I felt more awake than I had in months.

The music played as always, drifting through the station, sometimes in the background and sometimes all you could hear. The same songs over and over. The platform looked abandoned. I leaned back on the bench against the cool concrete and looked at the tracks bending away down that long corridor outside, towards Elephsina, Corinth, Belgrade, Venice, away to Pireaus. Athens was as good a place as any. And if I asked him outright he'd tell me. He would. He'd be the only one who'd really tell me. Straight up. He understood about this kind of thing. About facts. About a quick reply.

"Did you call Jezz's parents?" I asked.

He twisted his mouth and knit his eyebrows. "Of course I bloody called them. Thought you knew that, lass. Somebody has to be responsible. You would have if you'd been here." I nodded. He held my face in his hands again. "What is it?" His voice was coaxing, relaxed.

"Was it cause he was hurt?"

He laughed. I laughed a little too because it was a stupid question. He looked at his bare wrist and then nervously around the platform.

"We can talk about this after the run. I've got somethin special planned and I need to stay alert." He was still smiling at me.

"Listen, was it cause he was hurt?"

"You and I need a change of pace from Athens for a while, and after the run we can go to Argos and talk about whatever you want and we can make some plans."

"Okay," I said. "But did he get beat up? I know there were people who wanted to hurt him. I just want to know. Y'know, how it could have happened with you here. I just want to...."

"With me here?"

"Yeah, so tell me what...."

"You're ignoring me, lass." He raised his eyebrows. He bounced his knees up and down a little.

I smiled at him. "I really want to talk about it."

"Not. Bloody. Now."

"I read this thing...."

His smile was gone and he was struggling to talk nice to me. "Someone had to take responsibility for his life. It wasn't you was it? It wasn't Jack." In a moment he would be angry. I just wanted him to tell me and then I would shut up.

I nodded. "But was he hurt?" I asked.

He was angry now.

"Did he get a beating?" he sneered in an American accent. "Did someone hurt him and then make sure he didn't get to a doctor so that he'd die a few days later? Is that what you're asking? Did he have internal injuries that never got taken care of? Is that it?" His tone was utterly sarcastic, a horrible falsetto, and he kept smirking and blinking his eyes. He had obviously read the same article I had. He had the same information.

Then he smiled at me, a slow smile. "Did someone call his folks to get rid of his dying liability of a body? Is that what you want to know?" He raised his eyebrows. "That's the question, yes?" He grinned fiercely again, looked at me while I tried to figure out what he meant. He held my face in his hands, looked into my eye. A look that was a threat, then softened with a realization of its own, waited for me, guided me, brought me up that little trail between the words. He looked at me until I knew, and seeing it register on my face made him laugh. A light, delighted, genuine laugh, I tried to look down. He nodded at me, his eyes clear. "I did it because he was no good for you, luv," he said so straight and true. "And it was faster than an annulment. Y'did not love him. He wasn't good. I'd hate to see you live with that mistake for the rest of your life."

I couldn't have heard him right. I know I couldn't have heard it. The air took on a strange quality, became thicker. My whole body had that sensation your arm has when the cast comes off and it rises on its own. Floats.

I shook my head. I felt sick. If I opened my mouth it would all go wrong. He slapped me a few times on the knee, squeezed my shoulders again. "Ah, snap out of it. We'll get you a drink after the run. Here eat another cookie. These are good for you, they are."

It was definitely time to go. I would say I had to go to the bathroom and then leave. I would go to Drinks Time and then get a bus to England. I would get a boat back to Italy and....

Spero came on to the platform from the back gate. He was looking down the tracks too. Waiting for the tourists like the runners were. The other drivers stayed behind the gate where I could hear their voices mixed faintly with the music from the station.

"Here, hold these a second, lass. I gotta talk to him for a bit." He handed me his package of lemon cookies, stood up, and walked over to Spero. He looked over at me and grinned. I put a cookie in my mouth and tried not to look like I was about to run.

David sprayed his water bottle all over Spero's face and chest. Runners turned to see what was going on. The driver stepped back a few paces and clutched at his eyes. Then David's hand flashed from the pocket of his jean jacket and seemed to magically ignite the man. He shrieked as the flames engulfed his head. People jumped to their feet, most of them leaving as fast as they could, but some stayed to watch as fire consumed Spero's chest and arms, as he screamed running blindly and slapping himself and convulsing.

A few of the other drivers lurched forward from the gate and tried to grab him. They had taken off their shirts to cover him. But David stepped between them and Spero, who was shrieking in pain and horror, so he could guard the fire like it was his owner.

"Who's next?" he asked. Then he walked over to me and shook me furiously by the shoulders. "Stop screaming!" he yelled into my face. "Stop fucking screaming! Shut the fuck up. Now." He grabbed my head and put his hand over my mouth, held my nose. "Shut. Up!" he screamed, shaking my head, glaring into my face. "Shut the fuck up." Then he let go quickly. Sending my head into the brick wall. I took a deep breath and then the noise was only half as loud. Only the last of Spero's cries.

The fire grew bigger and started down his legs. He fell, shook, did not scream anymore. Thick sweet smoke curled over the tracks.

The other drivers were gone. David stepped back a few feet to watch the blaze. The only noise was Spero trying to keep breathing. I heard it in my veins. I could smell the fire, gasoline, fire, flesh, hair, and taste the lemon cookie in my mouth. He had stopped moving but he was still burning.

The few runners that remained were standing behind David, watching. He rubbed his hands together briskly and held them out, palms toward the blaze. Then he came back over to sit by me. "Did you see them run?" he asked.

"No."

He laughed and shook his head. "You shoulda seen your face!"

"Put him out, David."

"Ah, he'll go out by hisself."

By the time the 309 had arrived, he had, and the remaining runners boarded the train to Elephsina.

"Are you on?"

I shook my head.

"I'll see you around eleven, then," he said, squeezing my hand. "Get some coffee, relax." He looked at me for a while. "And put a sweater on when you get back to Olympos," he said. "And make sure you put your feet up, lass."

I nodded.

I watched him get on the last car and watched the train pull away. I didn't look over at Spero, but I could smell him in my throat. I stood up and walked through the station and out on to the street. It was still light. I walked back to Olympos, through the lobby and up the stairs while Sterious was talking to me. I felt that I should walk very slowly, and I did, all the way up the spiral staircase to my room.

"Oh," I said trying to breathe. The shakes came hard now.

I sat on the floor and put my head on the mattress. I could still taste the lemon cookies and feel them in my teeth. I trembled as if I were freezing.

"Oh God," I whispered, rocking on my knees with my face against the mattress. My teeth began to chatter. My nose began to bleed profusely and blood ran over my face and shirt and hands.

"Shhh," I whispered, but it was hard to breathe. I could taste blood and hear an ambulance in the distance, getting closer.

Shhh. Shut up. Get up now, c'mon, it's time to go. I walked to the sink and turned the water on and put my head under the tap trying to rinse my hair and face. I changed my shirt quickly. Do not be an idiot. You are not scared. You're not stupid. Get your bag. Let's go. Move out. Move. *Run.* I whispered. *RUN.* I screamed. But I just stood there.

I checked my bag for my passport, put it in the front pocket of my cut-offs.

Okay, I said, putting the bag over my shoulder. I wiped my face again with a shakey hand only to find my nose was still bleeding. My teeth were still chattering.

Okay.

Okay, now.

Okay, now.

Let's go.

30

"Collect call from Maya will you accept?"

"Yeah!"

"Hello?"

"Hey! Where are you?"

"Still in Greece. I'm leaving today."

"Slow down, I can't hear you. Are you okay, Maya girl?"

"Mmhm."

"Holy shit. You're not crying are you?" he laughed. "Cause if you're crying...I'll have to come there and kick your ass." I could hear him smiling. "Okay little bonehead?"

I heard my own fake laugh. "I just miss you."

"Now I know you're not okay. You need anything, girl of steel?"

"No."

"Well then suck it up, whatever it is."

I nodded.

"How's the sightseeing?"

"I was on the islands for a while. That was good. I met an old friend there. I went swimming."

"Where are you going?" He was talking slowly, relaxed.

"I'll decide at the port."

"You got to get me your new address, okay Maya?"

"Maya?" my brother's voice said again.

"Yeah?"

"I got to go, Bone. You gotta write to me okay? With a new address."

"Okay."

"Take care."

"You too," I said.

"Bye."

"Bye, li'l Bone. You be good. Be a good girl."

I hung up the phone and looked out the window of the OTE at the busy street, through the ghost of my own reflection. I stared at the little dirty cars going by, at my dark thin face, swollen and ugly. My cut-offs, boots, my horrible hair and stained t-shirt. I stared at my eyes. I thought for the first time in years how far away I was, how no one could reach me. How I didn't have it in me to go home even if I wanted to. I wiped the blood off my mouth, lit a cigarette, and walked to the street, towards the subway. Towards Pireaus. Then headed underground.

"Mom," I said, waiting for an answer on the dark platform. "Mom."

The train rushed in on a torrent of cold air and I stepped inside.

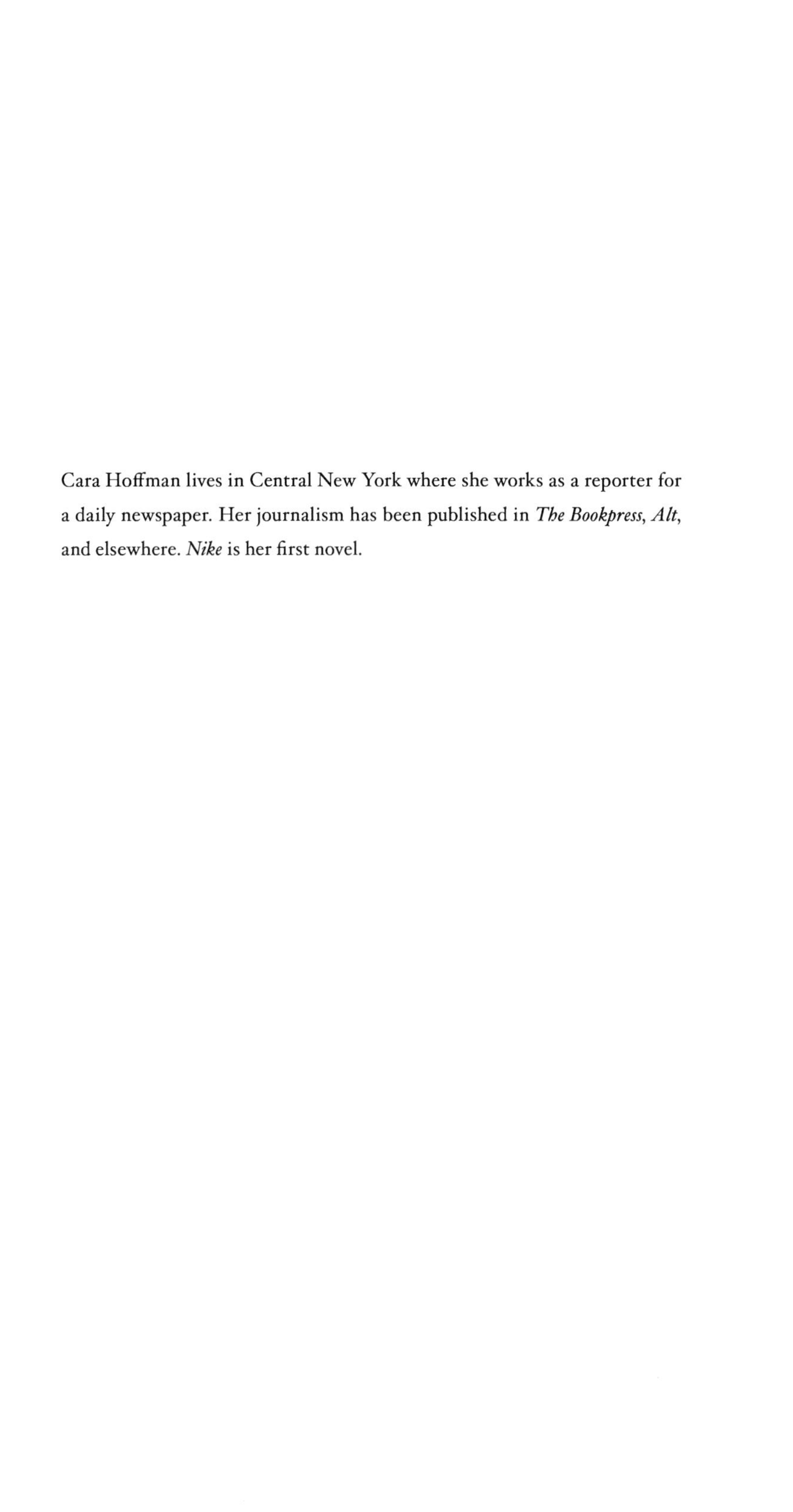

Cara Hoffman lives in Central New York where she works as a reporter for a daily newspaper. Her journalism has been published in *The Bookpress*, *Alt*, and elsewhere. *Nike* is her first novel.